Sobriety
And 49 Other Fine Stories

By Sarah Wolf

What do I do when my love is away?
(Does it worry you to be alone?)
How do I feel at the end of the day?
(Are you sad because you're on your own?)
No, I get by with a little help from my friends
Mmm, get high with a little help from my friends
Mmm, gonna try with a little help from my friends

The Beatles

FOR MY FAMILY

With the Following Special Acknowledgements

Tom Lada, Julia Ramus, Kim Freeman, Ben Folds, Sean OhEigeartaigh,
Devon Wilson-Hill, Shelby Finger, Kate Brigham, Rob Rogers, Shannon Robinson,
Anne Nolan, Dave Fertig, Tim Langan, Josh Hurd, Jennie Seigel, Karen Caiazzo, Jared
Bieschke, Justine Eachus, Nate DiNardo, Vinny Seigel, Chris Gray, Erin Good, Tina
Miller, Bill Anderson, Camilo Guaqueta, Holland Dieringer, Camille George, Bob
Hunsche, Lee Wesolowski, Sarah Bayle, Leslie Drescher, Erik Asmussen, and Joe Kay

who all contributed first lines that helped inspire the stories in this collection

To the Sun

She doesn't remember, but the last time she was here we made out. Tonight she's here with a young conventionally good looking guy. I bet his name's Dirk or Cato or something equally on the edge of pretension. Her name is Lily and she looks like she's on coke. She looks like the sort who maybe Dirk hired for the night. Maybe he did. When I kissed her, it didn't cost me a thing, though, so I don't pretend to know all the angles. I just sit here at this bar, night after night, and wonder who will sit down beside me next and if I'll want to talk or not. Some people really interest me. Lily interests me. She reminds me a little bit of my cousin Rachel. Rachel was always a little misunderstood and constantly running away from home. I wonder if Lily is a runaway. I bet she is. I stare at her in a loose fitting white top. It's backless and she's bra-less and it gets me thinking. She's got great arms, thin but muscular. I bet she does yoga. I bet she can climb trees. I see her fingers as they reach up and play through Dirk's curly brown hair. She's blonde and her hair hangs long and straight just past her shoulder blades. I watch as she slides her hand down to the back of his neck and pulls him into her. She kisses him with her eyes open. It's startling. I wonder if she kissed me with her eyes open. As she pulls back from him for a moment, her eyes sink solidly into his and then for a brief millisecond, she flashes those beautiful blues at me. Am I imagining it? I don't think so. Her smile shifts. Maybe she does remember.

I signal the bartender for another Jamesons on the rocks. His name's George. He's a good guy. He brings me my drink and juts his chin towards Lily. "Let her blow you sometime," he said with a wink. I nod slowly. Maybe I will.

"My man, good to see you," a new voice says beside me.

It's my friend Roy. We used to jam together in a band a few years ago. He still plays. I don't. At least not much.

"You on stage tonight?" I ask, signaling George to bring Roy the same thing I'm drinking.

Roy nods. "Sit in with us," he says. He always says that.

I smile politely. "Thanks, man, maybe." I always say that.

We clink our glasses together as soon as George sets Roy's drink down. "To the sun," Roy says.

Back in my music days, Roy and some of the other guys we jammed with hopped a plane for the tropics to see what the scene was like. Just thinking about those two weeks of suspended real-life brings back the feeling of sun on my face and a dull ache in my veins. It was fucking great. On the last night there, Roy and I were in a shitty little bar where everyone was trying -- quite successfully, I might add -- to sell us drugs and Roy stumbled into a girl -- a woman -- sitting alone at the bar. She told him her name was Jane, but I think she made that up. Anyway, Roy was trying to work some magic on her and I could see she was uncomfortable, so I turned his head towards another girl making waves on the dance floor and I took this strange Jane by the hand. It was an electric moment. It was like all we needed to do was press our palms together and our lifelines fused forever. The band was some kind of reggae hip hop workshop but I took sweet Jane and spun her around and then pressed her close to me. We swayed back and forth with our eyes locked into each other and moved slowly and deliberately and without any consideration for the music. Something came over me -- maybe it was just the intense heat of what we were doing -- and at the last moment, I dipped her low, her back arching towards the ground. I don't know what we looked like, but I felt like a fucking ballroom champion dancer at that moment. As I pulled lovely Jane back up to standing, I saw tears streaking down her face. "Thank you," she said to me. Thank you! And then she ran outside. I stood completely still for a moment before I chased after her. She hadn't gone too far, just outside the door. She told me her boyfriend had dumped her earlier that day. Left her for another woman. She lived on the island, she told me, and she had never wanted to escape from paradise more than she did that day and somehow my arms around her made a difference in her life. She brought me home with her and the next day, I got on a plane and came back to Somerville, Massachusetts. I wonder if her name really is Jane. I wonder that all the time.

"To the sun," I echo back at Roy.

Lily is positioned directly behind Roy so I can keep watching her move while I talk to him about his kids and his ex-wife. I don't have kids or an ex-wife. Listening to

Roy talk, I am thankful for both of those things. Instead, I have girls like Lily in my life. Looking around the room, I can count at least four men who have fucked her, Roy included. I haven't fucked her. Not yet, at least. Maybe I will. The night is young. Life is young. I order another Jamesons as Roy claps a hand on my shoulder and excuses himself to set up for the music. I fix my eyes on Lily but I do it in a non-creepy way. At least, I think that's what I'm doing. She doesn't seem to notice me. How could she? Her hands are busy working Dirk and her tongue is sweeping the inside of his mouth. I watch her jaw move. I like what I see. I remember what it was like to be Dirk. I hate that asshole.

I don't know if I'm drunk yet. It's hard for me to tell anymore. I wonder if it even really matters. I live two blocks from this bar so I'm within easy stumbling distance. I wonder if I should be looking for someone to stumble home with instead of fixating on Lily. But I can't stop looking at her. When she turns to the side, I can see part of her breast. I am staring now. This realization hits me and I feel like a predator, so I shift my gaze down into my rocks glass. When did I become *this* guy?

My girlfriend would roll her eyes at me if I asked her this question. She'd say, "*What* kind of guy do you think you are now? You're *a* guy, that's for sure." But she'd say it kindly, with her arms wrapped around my neck. Her arms aren't as nice as Lily's but they're nice enough. She's also not really my girlfriend. I call her that when she's not around because it best defines how I feel about her, but she's probably in a bar a few blocks away with her hand in some other guy's back pocket. I don't let my imagination run the full gambit. I know she winds up in beds besides mine but I can only picture her curled up next to me. She sleeps with her mouth wide open. It's wild. I love everything about her except for the fact that I know she's pressed up against some other man right now. Fact, I don't know that for a fact. But I let myself assume.

I let myself stare at Lily.

Roy and the boys are starting to play the first song. Lily and Dirk have suddenly vanished from sight. I think about George's endorsement -- *Let her blow you sometime.* Dirk, you lucky bastard. I turn my attention to the music. Reggae tonight. Roy's "To the sun" toast suddenly makes sense. I let my head move slightly out of time with the music. I wait to see who else will sit down beside me.

First line by Tom Lada

Wanda Leonard Fell in Love

She thought it was strange that no one looked up as she passed by his desk. Didn't they all know by now that she was sure to have an intense I-will-not-cry moment every time she saw his screen saver, a montage of wedding photos from his recent nuptials? Did they not care at all about her drama and suffering? Just to emphasize her plight, she rocked back a step and lingered with her hand resting on the back of his empty swivel chair and for extra measure she plucked a tissue from his very own supply to dab the corners of her eyes. With a hefty sigh, she watched the photos blink by for a few moments, immune to their true happiness vibe, and then turned slowly back towards her own desk a few cubicles down. Still, no one came to her aid, no one even noticed as she loudly blew her nose once back in her own chair. Staring straight ahead at the spreadsheets on her computer desktop, she grimaced. "What assholes," she muttered.

Wanda Leonard fell in love with Marc Arnold on August 22nd in the year of our lord 2009 and all of these office gnomes knew it. They were there, after all. Company bonding bullshit picnic. "Mandatory fun!" Don, the overly pleasant office manager declared. And Wanda wasn't one to succumb to such nonsense but there was this new guy who sat a few cubes down from her that caught her eye by the water cooler a few times and he seemed the type to like a company picnic so she figured, why not? Could be...fun. So she went and she was right -- the new guy with there, playfully messy brown hair and all -- and when it came time for games she ordinarily ran away from as fast as she could, she instead positioned herself close to this fine young man, strapping and strong and dressed in that devil-may-care fashion sense she so loved and managed to partner herself up with him for the company picnic's most hallowed event: The Three-legged Race. The minute he placed that, oh god, well toned arm strongly around her shoulder and she slid her own, well, not unattractive arm around his, she looked just the right degree up at him and her vision turned into Disney Princess mode: *this* was Prince Charming. Never mind that they tripped and fell to their knees about four paces in and came nowhere near to winning the race. Wanda was in love. As they untied themselves, he gave her a pained smile and said, "Maybe next year!" Before he could get up and walk away, she went with her impulse to give him a friendly little kiss, that, because it was impromptu and completely unexpected, landed near his right eye. "It's a date!" she said with her eyes a-flutter.

About a week later, she discovered his name was Marc when she waited for everyone to go home and then sunk deeply into his desk chair and touched all of his stuff, including his nameplate. After that every interaction she had with him became a Dear Diary moment – *Dear Diary, Marc bumped the wall on my cubicle today and you should have seen the smile he gave me when he said, "Sorry"... Dear Diary, Marc spilled coffee during a staff meeting and it trickled right towards me – could only mean one thing...* -- and before long, she realized there was no other end to this story than they two of them riding off together into the sunset.

And then Mallory Klein happened.

It was the week before the company picnic and Wanda was sitting at her desk, daydreaming about The Three-legged Race and planning her outfit when a pinch-faced work-neighbor called Tessie stuck her head around the cubicle corner.

"Psssssst. Wander!" Tessie whispered.

Tessie always mispronounced her name "Wander." It drove Wanda crazy beyond belief.

Wanda's dreamy gaze soured. "What?" she asked, turning towards the interrupting voice.

"Marc just changed his Facebook status."

Wanda froze as she stared at this intruding voice.

"He's *in a relationship*," Tessie went on.

Wanda remained still and silent.

"Look on Facebook -- it's true! Wander, he's gotta girlfriend!" A pause. "She's pretty, too," Tessie added, just to be spiteful, for sure.

Wanda felt her entire body start to quake, blood rushing everywhere, enough to institute a full body blush and then she erupted:

"WHAAAAAAAAAAAAAAAAAAAAAAAAAAAAT???????????????"

Everything in the office went silent for a moment and then there was a rustle of movement as people rubbernecked to see what had caused the outburst. Wanda was already on her feet, that was just her rage level, as she logged into Facebook and saw that pinch-faced Tessie was correct. "Marc Arnold is in a relationship with Mallory Klein."

Wanda immediately clicked to view Mallory Klein's profile.

"PRIIIIIIIIIIIIIIIIIVAAAAAAAAAAAAAAAAAAATE!" Wanda howled. "SON OF A BITCH." Still on her feet, Wanda stared at the thumbnail profile picture of the adorable redhead in the Braves t-shirt and tried to see into her soul. All she got was a broken heel on her shoe when she stomped her foot down. It was then that Wanda noticed everyone in the office had stopped what they were doing to watch her meltdown.

But instead of reacting to this realization like a sane person, Wanda felt empowered and limped her way down to Marc's cubicle.

"Who's Mallory Klein?" she asked.

Marc, who had also stopped his work to see what Wanda was screaming about, appeared shocked and terrified as she now hovered over him. "Mal's my girlfriend?" he managed after a few seconds of intense stare down.

"Your girlfriend," Wanda repeated. She leaned in close to him. "Perfect," she said.

And with that, she burst into tears and limped her way into the empty conference room where she remained alone for about twenty minutes until a very timid Office Manager Don and HR Representative Carmen came in and sat down across the table from her. By then, she wasn't crying anymore. She was sitting with her hands folded on the table, her chin resting on her forearms.

"Wanda, why don't you take the rest of the day off?" Don said after a moment of awkward throat clearing.

Wanda didn't attend the company picnic that year. Instead, she stayed home and started a blog about how much love sucks and clicked Mallory Klein's profile every few minutes, hoping against all hope that her privacy settings had changed since she last checked. But it never did. Not in the weeks and months that followed, either. In the meantime, her treatment of Marc Arnold turned pay-attention-to-me-cold and she flaunted her hatred of him and her broken heart as often as she could. Her co-workers feigned sympathy for awhile and then became increasingly annoyed, not that such a shift would deter her. Marc treated her like a breakable mask, keeping their interactions brief and strictly business. But every time he came near her, Wanda felt her chest tighten as her heart throbbed bigger than the cage she kept it in. Why did he have to be so goddamn adorable? It just made her want to sit at her desk and cry. And sometimes she did.

When Marc Arnold's Facebook status changed from "in a relationship" to "engaged," no one dared tell Wanda. They didn't have to -- she saw it herself within minutes of the update. She watched over the last year-plus as co-worker after co-worker became friends with this Mallory Klein -- Mallory Klein was even suggested as *someone she might know* since they had twenty friends in common. Wanda had never met her and Wanda was not invited to the wedding.

Now as she stared at the spreadsheets, she wondered how he and *Mallory* were enjoying their honeymoon. Marc had talked about nothing else for the previous two weeks -- how they delayed their honeymoon because Mallory was a school teacher (of course she was) but had wanted a May wedding so they could have the same anniversary as her grandparents who were married for seventy-eight years (of course they were) and how they were going to the same Hawaiian resort as those fabled grandparents and cutesy cutesy coo. Wanda had sat miserably at her desk and tried to tune out the sound of his musical, beautiful, sonorous voice, all the while trying to find pictures from the wedding on her co-workers Facebook pages. "Did those jagoffs block them from me?" she muttered. But just days before he left for Hawaii, Marc installed the screen saver montage so Wanda could see just how beautiful and happy that day had been. "Some people have all the luck," she sighed as she opened a new spreadsheet.

And when the phone on her desk rang a few minutes later, she answered it lazily and when Larry, her husband of seven years, asked her if she wanted duck or salmon for dinner that night, she said, "Duck," and hung up the phone.

First line provided by Julia Ramus

The Housewife

Last time she returned from Edinburgh, she brought me a plaster skull from a Fringe production of *Hamlet* and a postcard of a topless woman.

"For your collection," she's said vaguely, winking in my general direction.

"Thanks, Mom," I said, a moderate blush rising on my cheeks.

Ever since the divorce, she'd seemed bound and determined to add as much flash and ferocity to her life as was humanly possible, the classic ruffling of the housewife's housecoat. It's like, Dad left and now all of the sudden she'd discovered red lipstick and fishnet stockings. My mother, the burlesque dancer, jet setting around the world with her divorce settlement and a single overnight bag that must have the depth of Marry Poppin's carpet bag. My entire life, I never saw the woman leave the house without someone holding her hand, and now she can't be contained. For the first time in fifty years, she was living an independent life.

I was a grad student at Harvard studying English literature and it was not uncommon for my mother to show up on campus, out of the blue, toting goody bags like the Edinburgh haul. She'd taken an avid interest in my sexual identity -- lesbian to bi to lesbian to straight to bi to straight to lesbian once more -- and liked to pour bottomless glasses of wine into the wee hours discussing my love life, a topic that used to pucker her face up like a prune. It was partly refreshing and partly disconserting how accepting she was of my girlfriend Julie but I accepted that this was my mother's midlife crisis, not mine, so I should freely tell her whatever I could about my life so that when she snapped back to reality she'd at least have had the chance to be open minded about her baby girl.

"Agatha, I'm sorry I said you brought your women-friends to dinner with your father and me to be difficult. I see now how stuffy I was being," my mother would say as her head hit the pillow in my bed.

I'd scoop up her empty wine glass and pat her on the back as I left the room to return to reading Kafka.

She'd disappear from my life as easily as she popped back in it, so I got used to her knocking on my door at all hours and then not seeing her for a few months at a time. I would call my father occasionally and say, "Dad, have you talked to her at all?"

My father was reserved and, thus, of few words. He'd grunt at me and say, "Aggie, after twenty-five years together, we've got nothing left to talk about."

I'd sigh and hang up the phone and brace myself for the next sweeping visit.

Once after a four month absence, my mother reappeared, looking a little less spunky than I'd seen her on previous occasions, toting a bag full of Toblerone chocolate bars she said she'd picked up at Heathrow.

"You still like chocolate, Agatha, right?" she'd said, her voice a little lackluster.

"Mom, are you OK?" I'd asked.

"Fine, sweetie," she'd said, absently patting my hand. "Just ran into a little bit of trouble in London, that's all."

"What kind of trouble?" I asked.

"I got mugged," she said. "A man... He bullied me into an alley and demanded my money, everything."

I blinked. "What?"

"Luckily, I had left my passport in the safe at the hotel along with a bit of money. But everything else, he got all of it. My money, my credit cards, my cigarettes, my gum -- everything," my mother said.

I instinctively went to embrace her, but she gently pushed me back. "No, it's fine," she said. "I'd just forgotten why I'd been so prone to staying home all these years or only doing the safe things your father wanted the family to do. And then, with my back pressed against a wall and a threat of violence in my face, I remembered."

"Mom..." I began.

"No, it's really OK, Agatha. I just remembered. I remembered everything. Why a safe life was held with such high regard, why I stayed with your father more than a decade longer than I still loved him, why I never took chances before. Because this is what happens -- this is *life*. That's the reason I always hid behind closed doors, because what's out there -- here -- is scary. People are violent and desperate. My own daughter prefers the sexual company of women, an evolutionary conundrum. It's so much easier to stay quietly at home and be protected from all of these realities." My mother paused and then smiled softly at me. "After the man got what he wanted, I ran back to the hotel as fast as I could and I reported the incident and then I got my stuff from my room and hightailed it back to the airport. It wasn't until the plane was in the air that I felt safe at all but by the time we were at cruising altitude, I felt cowardly and foolish. I shouldn't have run away like that. I should have stayed in London and finished what I'd set out to do there."

"What was that?" I asked.

My mother locked eyes with me and said, "Prove that I am a woman. Prove that I am an individual. Prove that my experience will be meaningful and maybe even instructional. Prove that I am not an ambitionless housewife. That I can make it in the world -- literally -- the *world*. I look at you, my daughter, such a high academic achiever, going places, living a full, rich life that seems to make you happy and I am filled with love but at the same time shame because I know you didn't learn how to be that woman from me. Maybe someday you'll have children and I want them to look at me and be inspired, just as I am inspired by you."

She didn't let me get a word in edgewise in that conversation and left town abruptly afterwards and from that day on, she still packed her overnight bag and wandered off into the world alone, but now when she comes back with trinkets from her time away, I do my best to keep them in a safe place where they can be preserved and valued for many years to come.

First line by Kim Freeman

Thank You for Breaking My Heart

There was only one light on in the otherwise dark room and he'd been sitting nearly motionless since the last time the door closed. That had been awhile ago, long enough that the room had gone from the dusty glow of dusk to the black of night. He was just *there,* not doing anything, redefining his inner sense of numb, his hands flat on his bent knees, his eyes staring dully ahead, still in a protective over-her-head gaze, despite the fact that she'd left him there alone and therefore wasn't someone he needed to avoid any longer. When he blinked, he half-expected the scene to change, for light to flood the room and her loud presence to consume him once more. It's what he wanted. It's what would propel him forward instead of sitting, just sitting, in silence.

She wasn't inclined to give him what he wanted, though, and that was a fact he was keenly aware of in this looping moment.

There was a noise -- a faint buzzing somewhere nearby. He blinked a few times and realized it was his cell phone and he wondered where it was. He supposed it must be under a pillow somewhere, so he leaned over for the first time in a long time and found it under a blanket at the end of the couch. It was his sister calling. He opted not to answer. Instead, he distracted himself once more by getting up and walking around the room. Maybe his initial intent was to turn on more lights or flip on the television, but his feet took him directly across to the bookshelf where he found an old pink music box, the kind that had a ballerina to spring up from inside while it spun on a wobbly axis along while a nameless waltz churned in the air, and he did what he never had done before -- he opened the box and he closed his eyes for a moment to listen to the music. It crackled and stuck in places but the melancholy of the tune seemed to strike a physical blow against him.

This was something *she* used to do -- she used to open this box, one of her favorite belongings, something given to her by her grandmother, and make him listen, though he never really did, and now that he was, it made him feel light headed as he pressed his hand against the wall by the shelf. It made him feel simultaneously sick and hopeful -- this proved she would be back. She'd come back for this music box if nothing else.

But she won't come back for me, he thought with a quiet voice inside his head. *She'll never come back for me.*

He hadn't really known it until she'd walked out the door for the first time that he'd loved her at all. It might seem like an obvious thing, that a man would love his wife. It's practically the Western definition for a marriage bond. But after two years of courtship and three years of marriage, he'd never even considered it as an option or a necessary step in defining their relationship. She had assumed he'd loved her, that's what she said the first time she left him. She'd said, "I need more than just an affectionate business partner -- I need to feel that true bond -- I need to be with someone who is capable of love." And he'd let her leave that time because he couldn't think of a quick enough rebuttal. He couldn't put into words how love was something caged and unreleasable, criminal in his gut. Opening that door, throwing away that key, that wasn't something he would do, so maybe it was best for her to go if the sort of man she wanted was careless with his soul. And once she'd left, he missed her, it was true, but even then, he didn't think he loved her, though he wondered about it all the time.

His sister had called him up during that separation and said, "Don't be a fool. She's a good woman and she's good for you. You could be good for each other. Please, just work on it. You'll regret it if you don't."

But he ignored her advice and his wife came back on her own, her head cooled and her eyes hardened. She'd just showed up one night and said, "I have to believe in this," and he'd remained complacent and opened the covers for her to slip into their bed as if she'd never been away at all. As the days tripped along, though it was obvious that his wife had gone away and not fully returned. He could feel her detachment, like an untied shoelace on the foot of someone too busy to stop and fix the problem.

"Close that music box, I'm trying to think," he'd grumble on his more agitated days as his wife would flit through their apartment humming along with the song.

She'd sigh and only comply half of the time.

He was a musician by trade, a classically trained pianist who struggled to make a living as a rock-n-roll-star-slash-piano-teacher, and he was certain this is the only reason his wife had become such at all. They'd met casually a few times when his band played a bar where her brother worked as the manager and they'd gotten to know each other one night after a gig when she'd had just enough gin and tonics to saunter up to him and sit down beside him at the keyboard.

"I like what you do," she'd said, her smile unbearably wide.

He'd surveyed her, flicked his eyes over to where her brother tended bar, and started playing George Harrison's "Something" as a response to her statement.

"That's my favorite song," she'd whispered when he finished.

"It's every girl's favorite song," he'd shrugged. "What else do you like?"

And they'd played that game until long after the bar closed, long after the other bandmates had packed up their gear and left, only making a final exit when her brother came over and waited patiently for him to finish the Ben Folds song "Time" before clucking out the most famous bartender wisdom known to man -- "You don't have to go home but you can't stay here."

He'd raised a curious eyebrow at this girl's brother who'd shrugged as his sister nuzzled against him. "She's had a crush on you for awhile, dude. Just be good to her, that's all."

Just like that. A blessing. He took the girl home with him and nothing in his life changed except that now she was there all the time.

"It's unreal, you know," she'd said once after she'd taken him back the first time. "I listen to you play the piano and sing the songs you wrote for me and what I hear and see and feel in those performances is something raw and pure, something I would call true love. But when the song's over, it's just over." She'd pause and look at him as he'd avoid looking directly at her. "How do you *do* that? How do you turn it off and on like water?"

He hadn't known what to say, so he'd left the room and sat down to work on a new composition. Later that night in bed when he was sure she was already asleep, he'd finally offer some sort of response. He'd say, "I try," but she never heard him.

This time when she left, he could feel it was for real. She'd stood in the living room and smiled sadly at him and said, "I gotta go."

He swallowed hard. "What can I do?"

"Nothing," she said, her usually loud voice barely a whisper.

He wanted a different answer so he asked her once again. "What can I *do*?"

She'd brushed away a tear and tried to meet his avoiding stare. "Goodbye," she said and she walked out the door.

So then he'd sat there, doing nothing, waiting for something to seize him, and nothing did until he listened to that music box. His hand pressed so hard against the wall that his knuckles were white and the sound of that waltz flooded his brain. He listened to it over and over until it slowed down so much it was barely plucking out notes. Only then did he close the lid on the box. Only then did he leave that dimly lit room and sit down at his piano. Only then did he reconstruct that waltz on his own terms. In the stillness of that dark night, he played that melody and began to sing, "*Thank you for breaking my heart. Now at least I know that it is in there.*" He had left it wide open without even knowing it and now it was the end. With his head hanging over the bright white ivory keys, he played the waltz over and over, without slowing down, without losing pace with the beating of his heart.

Inspired by the Ben Folds Five song of the same title

The Brothers

"Well, what do *you* do on your day off?"

"I work."

"And that's the problem."

The brothers took simultaneous sips of coffee and clanked them back on the table in perfect, unplanned unison. Had they been fifteen years younger, they would have appeared as mirror images sitting across from one another in this diner booth, but Gary was *overfed*, his own euphemism, while Yorick was gaunt and pale, *like the skull he was named after*, his own euphemism, and their ability to sell themselves as the biological twins that they were became more difficult over time.

"Remember when Dolores couldn't even tell us apart?" Gary would sigh, referring to his wife of twenty-two years.

"Sure do," Yorick would say with a slightly evil glint in his eye.

Life had safe-guarded Dolores from making that mistake again. But that was also a euphemism.

The brothers sat across from each other not eating their pancakes but instead waiting stubbornly for one of them to get to the reason Gary had called this breakfast meeting on a Saturday before he went into the office. They had bigger fish to fry than nitpicky details about what they chose to do with their days off and both men knew it.

Gary crumpled up his napkin and tossed it on the table.

"I guess I'll go first," he said.

Yorick didn't even blink. "OK," he said.

"I don't care about what happened to the car," Gary began.

"I told you I'd pay for the damages," Yorick interjected.

"And you will, no doubt. But that's not the issue," Gary said in a slow, calm voice.

"I'll pay for it as soon as I can. I already apologized to Suzie," Yorick said.

"Suzie isn't the issue either," Gary said, a frown involuntarily overtaking his face as he recalled his daughter's devastation over the wreckage that once was her eighteenth birthday present.

Yorick's cool began to crack. "I already said I'm sorry for what happened."

"And we have accepted your apologies and your offer to fix the car," Gary said patiently. "But the issue is bigger than what happened after Suzie's birthday party. It's bigger than what happened during Suzie's birthday party. It's bigger and you know it so stop interrupting me and let me get this out."

Yorick's eyes flashed and he swallowed hard. "I have a right to defend myself," he said.

Gary raised his eyebrows at this and then laughed dryly. "Yes, I suppose you do," he said, a little amusement in his voice. "But let me say what I need to say before you start defending yourself against it."

Yorick slouched in his seat and didn't respond.

"You showed up high to your nieces's eighteenth birthday party," Gary said softly. "I'm guessing, what, coke? And then you served her underage friends whiskey shots and then, without asking, you took the keys to the brand new car that Suzie had helped pay for and you tried to drive your intoxicated self to the liquor store when you sped through a heavy traffic intersection, causing a three-car accident before you slammed into a parked car, an incident that resulted in your third DUI, which means when your case goes to trial you *will* go to jail. And if the judge finds out you were also illegally serving minors, you're in real deep shit." Gary paused, his voice still even and calm. "We don't care about the damage to the car," he added, his eyes locked on his brother's.

Yorick looked away and stared at his uneaten plate of food. "I said I'd pay for the damages," he muttered.

"Yeah, yeah, Yor, I know," Gary sighed, sipping his coffee.

When they were kids, Gary was the popular one. He made friends easily and he excelled at sports. He charmed all the women and was effortless at anything social, making it no great surprise that he went into public relations and politics in college. Yorick had a harder time socially. He was always a little odd and his misguided name choice didn't help things -- "You couldn't have just named me Larry?" he used to moan to his mother, a huge Shakespeare buff who'd stuck him with this *Hamlet* character reference. While Gary was Mr. Popular, Yorick excelled in academics, particularly math and science, and while Gary was the Prom King, Yorick was Valedictorian. While Gary went to University of New Hampshire, Yorick went to MIT and they both had successful college runs. Finally, Yorick was among the socially awkward and it was OK to be as such. He found friends who showed him the magic of ecstasy and acid, never mind gin and tequila, and he realized why these exceptionally smart people found such comfort in these substances he'd been taught his entire life to avoid: they slowed down his rapidly firing brain. They made him feel less odd. They calmed his unrelenting anxiety and he thought to himself, "Maybe this is what normal is like." And by the time Yorick and Gary returned to their parents' home for their first summer break, Yorick was already in a state of being high all the time, something their parents seemed to ignore but threw Gary for a loop. And when Gary found out why Yorick's behavior was altered, Yorick had sworn his brother to secrecy, something Gary did but regretted every day. Yorick seemed happy and that was something no one in their family had ever experienced, so they all accepted this new version of an old soul and let it go at that.

But at some point, it goes beyond substance abuse. At some point, it becomes disease. Gary had watched Yorick through his party years, still getting A's at MIT and moving straight into a high profile government job that had him in weapons research where he was eventually fired for getting stoned in the lab but his anguish over that was temporary since another private sector agency scooped him up and that's where he stayed for the next decade-plus before his first DUI, an incident that turned somewhat scandalous when he was caught at the scene of the crime with his boss's sixteen-year-old daughter in the car -- and it was obvious they weren't going out for ice cream. Even so, he was adopted by another private sector job and that's how it was for Yorick -- no matter how many times or ways he screwed up, his brilliant academic mind was irresistible and he was always in demand. Gary used to sit back and marvel at how backwards it all seemed -- this drunk coke head who looked like an AIDs-ridden homeless person with a scorecard of DUIs was actually one of the global leaders in his field -- Einstein-level stuff. Nothing seemed to teach Yorick not to be anything but the way he was because even when there were consequences, there really were no consequences.

"Remember when we were kids and I wanted to be an astronaut and you told me I'd suck at it because I'm claustrophobic and afraid of heights?" Gary asked, finally cutting into his pancakes.

Yorick raised an eyebrow at his brother. "Sort of," he said.

"Come on, your remember. You must. Because I responded in a very specific way," Gary said, almost jovially as he chewed with his mouth a little open.

"You punched me in the face and knocked out my front tooth," Yorick said dryly.

"Exactly. I knew you'd remember," Gary said.

"So what about it?" Yorick asked.

"So you were right and I responded irrationally and with violence," Gary said, his tone shifting to a more somber tone.

"Who cares, we were kids," Yorick said.

"Right, we were kids. But it was still a dick move on my part. Especially because you were right," Gary said. "That incident always stuck with me and I think it's why I've never punched you in the face when you've showed up in my home high."

Yorick sat up a little straighter and then slouched once more. "Yeah?" he asked.

"Yeah," Gary said. "I've wanted to punch you in the face pretty much every days since I caught you smoking pot in Mom and Dad's basement that first summer."

"But then I offered you a hit and it mellowed you out?" Yorick asked, weakly attempting humor.

Gary grimaced. "I should have never lied for you, Yor."

"But you did and that was forever ago so who cares?" Yorick asked.

"I wonder if I could have... helped you," Gary said.

Yorick laughed and shook his head. "Helped me do what? Man, you didn't do anything. It wouldn't have mattered if you had ratted me out -- I wouldn't have stopped. I liked being high -- I still like being high. Being sober makes my skin crawl, it makes my brain overload. I can't relax, I can't talk to people, I can't do anything but live inside my head and try to address every anxiety that crowds in. I don't want to be sober, not even now, not even though it means I'll have to go to jail. I can still get high in jail, so it doesn't matter. I'm an addict -- yeah, I've taken that first step in admitting the problem but the solution, the cure is worse than the disease. So, yes, I'm sorry about the damage to Suzie's car and I will pay for it. But I won't be doing anything else and I know you don't agree with that or respect it -- or probably me -- in any way, but I also don't give a fuck. I'm the one who has to live in this body and this is how I cope." Yorick fished a twenty dollar bill out of his wallet. "So if you don't mind, I'm going to go and enjoy my day off by not working," he added, throwing the money on the table and scooting out of the booth.

"What if I can't be supportive anymore?" Gary asked without turning his head.

Yorick paused, also not turning around. "Then I understand," he said, walking out the door without looking back.

First line by Sean OhEigeartaigh

Ghosts

Something tells me I should never have come here. Everyone's smiling at me as if I've returned from the dead, and maybe, in some ways, I have. I stand awkwardly in the doorway and no one says anything for the longest split second of my life before Mr. Burton breaks the silence with a, "Here here!" and someone hands me a glass of champagne. "The returning hero!" Jerry says, clapping his hand across my back and ushering me to the center of the room.

My mother must be somewhere nearby -- she's responsible for all of this. She'll emerge from the mist as only she can and until then, I'll have to suffer in silence alone. I don't want any of this.

Miss Sofia and her little yorkshire terrier Sue are at my side and she's grabbing my wrist with the hand that's not supporting her dog.

"Should I call you Sarge still?" she asks in one of those old lady voices that borderlines between intense sugar rush and creepy.

"Sure, Miss Sofia, I still go by Sarge," I say, flashing her a quick smile.

"I wasn't sure since you're a captain if that's what you'd want us to call you now," she continues, her grip on my wrist starting to shake. "Captain far outranks sargent."

"Yes, I know, but you can still call me Sarge," I say, gently pulling my hand away from her bony fingers.

"Well, I wanted to make sure," she says.

I want to ask if she remembers my real name but I doubt she does. I doubt anyone in this room does, except for my mother, wherever she's hiding. I was named after my mother's grandfather Sergio, but someone started calling me Sarge as a kid and it stuck and it became increasingly ironic after I joined the Marines out of high school. That was a decade ago, though, and after tours in Iraq and Afghanistan, I had lost my sense of irony. I left it on a plane somewhere, I think.

"Sarge, we're so happy you're home," says the pretty voice of Mary Grayson, my high school crush-turned-soccer-mom-the-size-of-a-Winnebego. I can see her husband Dale over at the food table filling his plate with shrimp and cocktail sauce. She's got their youngest child Abigail slung in the crook of her arm while the two older ones swarm their father.

"Thanks, Mary. How old's this one?" I ask, nodding towards the sleepy-eyed youngster.

"A year and a half," Mary croons. "Your mother sent you pictures, right?"

I nod. My mother always keeps me abreast of what's up with Mary and any of my other old girlfriends still hanging around Montpiel, New Hampshire. I'm pretty sure she wishes I'd knocked up really any one of them and never joined the military to stick around town and be a dad. My eyes drift to Dale as he swats the older kid's hand away from his shrimp plate. No, thanks.

"Great to see you, Sarge," Mary says, her eyes following my drift towards her husband's station at the food table.

I kiss her on the cheek as a way to release her back into the wild, off to forage for her dinner like the suburbanite that she is.

"Sarge, great to see you back on safe soil," says Mr. Lewis, my mother's next-door-neighbor. He's shaking my hand rather vigorously. He's making me teeth chatter.

"Thank you, sir," I say, releasing his grasp.

He's folding his arms across his chest and he's sucking in a deep hiss of air. "S'not like my day, boy-o, this military stuff. In my day, you got drafted and sent off to war and when you came back, no one would speak to you. There sure were no parties in your honor, that's for sure."

I stare at him blankly. "No, sir," I say.

"Anyway, nice of your mother to put this together. We're awful proud of you, son," he says, unfolding his arms to offer a lightening fast salute before walking away.

My eyes follow him and my feet start to, as well, but I'm stopped almost immediately by Mr. Barton, who shouted *Here here!* upon my arrival.

"Sarge, we've been praying for you every Sunday at the church," he says, his eyes watery and kind. "You and all the other fellas -- fellas and gals -- serving overseas. Or serving at all. We pray for all of you."

"Thank you, sir," I say, the left corner of my lip raising in a half smile, the only genuine facial expression of happiness I make.

"And I ask Mrs. Burton up on heaven to keep an eye on you, too. All you fellas and gals in the military, sure, but mostly you. I feel OK asking her for special favors, you understand," Mr. Burton said, elbowing me jovially in the ribs.

"Yes, sir," I say, my half smile remaining.

"She always said you were special, you know that?" he continues. "Even as a little boy, she used to say to me, 'Albert, Sarge Bakerson is going to be an extraordinary example for others,' and you know what, she was right on the money. And God thinks so, too -- we all been prayin', but He's the one in charge."

The left corner of my mouth drops to form a straight line across. "Yes, sir," I say.

"For he's a jolly good fellow," Mr. Burton says with a wink as he squeezes my elbow and walks away.

I realize I've been standing in the middle of my mother's living room this entire time now without moving and I'm wondering where my brother David is. He's the one who dragged me here and shoved me through the door so he could stay outside and smoke a joint.

"How can this be scarier than war?" he'd asked before the door closed to separate us.

Looking up, I am reminded that this can be very scary, though in a different way than war. "Hello, Laurel," I say to the curvy blonde in front of me.

She's not saying anything and my palms instinctively start to sweat. My mother never sends me updates about this particular ex, but that's mostly because I'd asked her to marry me once and she'd said no, so my mother had declared her dead to our family. Yet here she is, standing in front of me.

"Sarge," she says, her brown eyes searching my dark green ones.

"Surprised to see you in my mother's house," I say, my throat feeling dry. I take a quick swig of my champagne and it doesn't help at all.

Laurel laughs and it sounds like a light rain -- pleasant if not slightly inconvenient. "Seems I'm back from the dead," she says.

"Me, too," I say, downing the rest of my glass and then setting it on the coffee table.

"Just a couple of ghosts, eh?" she teases and I instinctively look down at her ring finger to see if it's banded or not. It's not.

"I'd heard from David that you'd gotten married last year," I say.

"Never believe rumors from beyond the grave," she says with a shrug. "Ghost stories are meant to scare you."

I have stood in full battle gear and fired my weapon across enemy lines and yet standing in front of this woman in this moment is making my insides turn an uncomfortable mixture of rubber and water. "Yes, ma'am," I say, resorting to a rhetoric that feels comfortable.

"You look good, Sarge. And I would very much like to kiss you later, so please don't escape without including me in your plan," she says lightly as she turns and walks away.

This is a dream. I am dreaming. I have died and this is some kind of trick before heaven.

"She is still the hottest girl I ever banged," says a voice in my ear, jolting me back to earth.

"Shut up, David," I mutter, that half smile returning.

That is another reason our mother had previously banished Laurel from our lives -- in addition to breaking my heart, she also broke my little brother's a year after when they'd run into each other in Boston and had a four month fling that ended badly for David and took him another year to admit had happened at all.

"What's she doing here?" I ask.

"Pretty sure she's here to see me," he says wryly.

Laurel had broken up with him after admitting that the entire reason she'd hooked up with him at all was because he and I had the same eyes and the same voice, a truism for all the males in our family, and when she'd *come to her senses* (her words), she'd realized it was unfair to string David along. I'll admit that when my brother had first confessed the affair, I'd been pretty pissed off -- until the humiliating conclusion of the story. Then I just felt bad for the kid -- and sorry for Laurel, too. The signals of attraction could be so confusing sometimes.

"How'd she get invited?" I ask.

"I invited her, of course," David says. "I thought if she could see us standing side-by-side, she'd see who the real man of the family is."

My half smile remains. "Yes, sir," I say. "And Mom didn't freak out?"

David shrugs. "She doesn't exactly know..."

"Where *is* Mom, anyway?" I ask.

"She's around," he says evasively.

"Was she smoking a joint with you outside earlier?" I ask.

He grins at me. "Maybe."

"Sarge, welcome home!" says a new voice at my side.

"Let me go get you a beer," David says, walking away and leaving me with the next well-wisher.

The next few hours run like this: *Welcome back, Sarge, we're so proud of you and your service to your country and we're so happy you're safe and home and so on and so forth.* At no point does anyone ask me any of the details of war. No one wants to know what services they're specifically thanking me for. No one wants to know what it's like over there. No one asks to hear a story about my time overseas. No one asks me for my opinion. They all say *thanks* and move on down the line. I say my own brand of *you're welcome* and let them pass by. I am like a living memorial that these people have come to visit. If I were a a statue, they might even leave flowers at my feet. They are all friends and neighbors -- people who have watched me grow up. But we are foreign to each other now. We are on different levels of existence. They are showing such respect for the dead -- for me, for the Sarge they once knew, who is no more. They are thanking me for his service and I am gracious.

It's late in the game before I finally see my mother, red-eyed and slow-moving, so unlike the woman I remembered from my previous life. She'd been a strict and fierce parental force in my childhood and remained as such in my adult years, but my time overseas had weighed heavily on her. She'd always been the sort to unwind with a glass of wine, but both she and David had increased their self-medication in my absence. I am sitting on the couch between Jerry and his wife Kris and they're each patting me on a knee as they tell me how proud they are of me when my mother catches my eye.

"Excuse me," I say, getting up and moving towards her.

"Sergio, you're looking tired," she says, wrapping her hands around each cheek as she turns my head from side to side.

"Some party you put together here, Mom," I say.

She looks absently around the room. "Your father would have told me not to do it," she says with a sigh. "But his absentee vote didn't arrive from heaven in time for me to cancel."

My half smile perks up my face. "Mrs. Burton probably interfered," I say with a wink.

My mother's face softens and she hugs me close. "Those angels work together in mysterious ways," she concedes. "I hope it isn't too terrible."

"It's nice to see so many people," I say in a neutral voice.

"Yes," my mother says. "Even that woman who's dead to me is here, skulking around, waiting to pounce."

I chuckle. "Seriously, Mom, we're grown men..."

My mother pinches my cheek. "I will kill anyone who hurts my boys," she says. "Even if only metaphorically."

We both glance over and see Laurel in deep conversation with David. "Welcome to the haunted party," I say.

"Where else would you rather be?" my mother asks. Then her voice booms. "Everyone, stop what you're doing and raise your glass in honor of my son Sarge."

The room falls silent as glasses extend in the air.

"We can never honor enough your commitment to the widely-shared wish for a peaceful world. Bless you, son, and bless those still on the crusade," she says.

"Cheers," says one person after another.

I stand in the center of this world and feel overwhelmed by my mother's over-simplification of the last decade of my life and I am struck by the thought that the reason these scenes are so nightmarish for me is I know that one day, I will not be able to stand quietly by with my glass extended in the air -- I will need, *need*, to tell the world what I've seen and what I've done in the name of my mother's eloquently phrased mission of *peace*. Not being here means not having to make a decision to tell the truth or to remain quiet. It's the quiet that is killing me over and over, that has left me just another ghost in this haunted room. No one gives out Purple Hearts for these kinds of wounds.

First line by Tom Lada

Truth

It was the Judy Smith Smith Library because you know, like, she married her cousin. At least, that's what I tell the freshman who live on my floor in the Joan A. Bark Hall dormitory. Freshman, shit, they'll believe anything. When I was one, my RA told me that they put laxatives in the mashed potatoes and that the university president was once a Playboy bunny and who was I to say nay? Maybe all of those things are true, anyway. The Judy Smith Smith Library gag was old as the hills, though, and I honestly have no idea if it's true or not. Sometimes I stand in the library's entryway and stare at her portrait and I try to decide if she seems like the sort who'd consort with a blood relative. Something in her stare's a bit pervy. Maybe it is true.

True or not, it's what I tell all the freshmen who live on my floor in JAB Hall. I also tell them that the other reason we call it JAB is there was a famous fight in the common room between a girl who was French royalty and the heiress to the Hershey chocolate fortune once in, like, the eighties. I made that one up myself, but it spread like wildfire anyway so we keep up the tale. All of the other RA's started telling their freshmen about it and next thing you know, blame-o, we've got a bona fide rumor all of our own making. Feels good, to tell you the truth.

I also liked to tell people that my boyfriend Paulo is coming for the weekend and that my "do not disturb" sign is to be taken at absolute face value, which is bullshit because I haven't got a boyfriend named Paulo. I have a girlfriend, though, named Paula who could pass as a dude if you weren't paying close attention. I'm not sure I am actually a lesbian, see, that's why I don't drape my girl in a rainbow flag and parade her up and down the hall for all the frosh to see. It is none of their business -- it is barely even my own business. I just like the company, really.

After four years at this university, I'd learned a thing or two about what kind of company to keep and who to tell what to and when to let sleeping dogs lie. I try to teach the freshmen about this, too -- not to trust people at their word -- to ask questions. And I teach this lesson by lying to them repeatedly about pretty much everything. Shit, they all have computers and iPhones and trust funds -- they could find the answers if they were less lazy and more curious about the world around them. It took almost no provocation for me to flip into *teach-em-a-lesson* mode. If one of them came to me and said, "Astrid, like, I checked and Judy Smith Smith wasn't married to her cousin -- it was her second cousin," I would pat them right on the head and hand them a cookie. An actual cookie. I kept them in stock in my room just for such occasions.

But I almost never gave anyone a cookie.

I would curl in bed with Paula on rainy Sunday mornings and complain to her about the lack of interest in today's youth. "Why don't they give a shit -- any shits? Why do they just nod and say 'huh' and accept everything without question? I should make them all watch *Wag the Dog* and then they'd maybe learn to open their goddamn mouths."

Wag the Dog, by the way, is a film from the 90's about a president who fakes a war to distract from news that he had an illicit affair with a girl scout. It's brilliant and if you haven't seen it, you're a moron who probably believes that every six years the university hands out scholarships for the top three people who run the most laps on the rec center's indoor track.

That rumor isn't mine, but it's a personal favorite, largely because I fell for it my freshman year.

Anyway, Paula has no answers for me, but she usually distracts me from bitching and moaning by french braiding my hair, so, I can put a check in the win column.
And to tell you the truth, a win is probably better than the truth. One look at all these uneaten cookies, and that's all it takes to convince me that curiosity is its own kind of reward.

First line by Devon Wilson-Hill

Balance

I prefer to do standing balances in public restrooms. This only works, by the way, because I never wear high heels. Flip flops or Vans or sneakers or barefoot. Those are the options. But one of the many benefits of this footwear preference is I can keep my mind off of the fact that I am, for one reason or another, waiting in a bathroom. Waiting for a stall, waiting for my friends, waiting for something, always. I usually stand in Figure Four, slight bend in one knee while the other foot hooks around that knee so my legs literally look like a the number four. I used to do Tree pose, standing with one foot pressed into the other upper thigh, until my friend Jill pointed out how dirty the floor was and now I was infusing those grimey germs into the cheap apolstery I'd slung about my body that is otherwise known as my wardrobe. So now it's Figure Four with my hands pressed at heart center or nothing. All this means is I spend way too much time in public bathrooms.

I work part time in a retail store called Marigold's which sells Stuff That Forty-year-old Women Desperately Want to Buy. Pricey candles, picture frames with a thousand bedazzled rhinestones, oversized cardigans with things like cardinals and sleeping orange cats on them, lamps with shades draped in lavendar fringe. You can find us in the mall next door to Things Remembered. Jill used to work here, too, until she got an internship with the local NBC news affiliate. Now she gets a lot of coffee for wise-cracking morning anchors who actually seem to be pretty nice to work for, even though she has to be to work at the goddawful hour of, like, four a.m. News doesn't sleep, I guess. I'm sleeping then, though. If I'm working, I usually don't come in until noon-ish. It's the benefit of being part time and unimportant for all things except covering the manager's lunch break which she takes promptly at 2:15 p.m. every single day. When I'm behind the register, I usually stand in tree pose. The floor is carpeted so I'm not worried about the grimery germs in here. I like that no one sees me standing on one leg, that they think I'm just the run-of-the-mill bored part time retail sales associate, rolling eyes and sucking on a piece of hard candy since gum is not allowed. I'm not run of the mill, though, and these people, they'll never know it.

I guess the people I see in public restrooms, they might have a notion that I'm a little on the quirky side. But they mostly keep their eyes unfocused and do what they've come to do. One afternoon, I stood in Figure Four -- alternating balancing legs -- in the mall's food court bathroom for a solid hour. I just wanted to see who, if anyone, would ask me what the hell I was doing. You know what? Only three people did, all of them under the age of five -- and their mothers immediately *shh*'d them so I didn't even get to answer them. How messed up is that? I tried my experiment again, but for maybe only twenty minutes or so, at the Starbucks on Wilson Boulevard. Again, no one said anything to me, except the assistant manager who came in and asked me to leave after a snitch ratted me out. I didn't try the experiment again. But I still stood in standing balances while I waited the reasonable amount of time in the bathroom.

Jill said I should try to get a better job, or at least a full time job, and she also said I should work on different arm variations when I stood in my Figure Four. Heart center is but one option, after all. There's above the head, there's steeple grip, there's palms flipped up, there's forward folding, there's leaning to the side, there's twisting. Jill says I'm stuck in a rut. I think she's probably right.

One afternoon, I was standing in tree pose behind the register at Marigold's when the actor Bill Murray came in the store. I swear to God -- it was actually him. I observed him casually, wondering what his inner forty-year-old-woman would find appealing in this store. He picked some things up and smelled a few candles and spun the racks of greeting cards, selecting a few to read, chuckle over, and return to their slots. Our muzak was on the fritz that day and no one else was around, so the store was totally silent except for whatever noises actor Bill Murray was making as he made his way around. Then it happened -- he picked up a smooth round paperweight with the image of a butterfly stamped in the center (whole sale value: negative ten dollars; retail value, fifty-five) and he put it in his coat pocket. Actor Bill Murray looked over at me and smiled a sad, familiar smile, and said, "No one will ever believe that this happened." And then he walked out the door.

He was right, no one did. I told my boss and she sent me to go dust something and even Jill said, "Everyone knows the gag is he eats a french fry off your plate." I didn't make it up, though. It happened. Actor Bill Murray shoplifted from Marigold's while I stood by in Tree pose and did nothing about it. The thing I remember most vividly about the whole thing is that smile he gave me. It looked like *my* smile, as if life was an inside joke that we were both tired of understanding.

On my days off, I practice yoga in a park near the apartment Jill and I share just off the campus from where we both earned our bachelors degrees. I use a mat that's a green more brilliant than the grass and I stand barefoot at the top of it and start each sequence with a full Sun Salutation before doing a variation on Primary Series that swaps out a lot of the forward folds and most of the vinyasas for extra standing balances -- like Dancer or Warrior Three or Eagle -- and it always happens that I lock into the zone and when I settle myself down for Savasana, I open my eyes to realize that someone has stopped in his or her tracks to watch me. Dumbfounded. Like, what is *that* girl doing. Like, what sort of *religion* is she selling. You have to see their faces, I guess, to know what I mean, but they are confused by what they've just witnessed. It always brings that Bill Murray-esque smile to my face because all they've done is witnessed me being me, doing my thing, not bothering anyone, trying to find a little sense of balance in my meloncholy world.

First line by Shelby Finger

Siren

"More often than not, when I come to 5 Tannery, I'm in costume," she said.

He looked her over carefully from her long neon pink wig to her glittery purple butterfly wings to her white and silver tutu over a billowing tie dye skirt and, finally, her silver elfin shoes. "What are you supposed to be?" he asked cautiously.

She grinned at him and then leaned over and kissed his nose. "I'm me, silly," she said, spinning away.

He watched her disappear into the club, her neon hair sparkling in the dark, and he was unsure of what to do. And did she just kiss him? Everything about this girl was a blur to him. He wasn't even really sure how they met or how she'd gotten him to give up his phone number or how she managed to convince him to leave his studio apartment to mingle with the night. He didn't remember agreeing to any of this, yet here he was, out on the town. On a Tuesday, no less. How long had he known her? How long would this go on? He hovered near the door to 5 Tannery, a place he'd only read about on the internet until this moment, and watched what he decided must be a rave go on. This girl he was with, she wasn't the only one *in costume*, as she called it, but she was certainly the most flamboyant about it. As she worked through the room, she appeared to know almost everyone she saw, as evidenced by her effort to stop and hug and twirl with the body before her. He hugged closer to the door, dressed in faded blue jeans and a button down white shirt and wondered if she even remembered he was there. She had invited him, right? Is that how he wound up here? It must be what happened. This was not, after all, his scene. He felt so uncomfortable and grew increasingly so with each passing moment. It was almost like the looser the cavorters became, the tighter he was, tucked so far in a corner now he was very nearly vermin, cowering. But he didn't leave. And he didn't know why. Instead, he watched the room, attentively, almost thirsty for whatever hydrated these people. Especially her. She owned this place by not claiming it as her possession. He'd never seen anything like it and it both terrified and lifted him.

After what seemed like hours, she finally circled back to him, proving to himself that she had actually invited him here, and drew him into the middle of the crowd without a word. He let himself be led. He let himself be loose. Once he was there, in the pulsing heart of it, there was nothing to stop his hips from swaying, his arms from jabbing at the air. She spun around him like a top, her wings and her skirt and her wig flying. He was part of this now, part of this scene, part of her. Just like that. He tipped his head towards the ceiling and let his jaw hang slack. He was stunned -- this was stunning. Drawn into the center of the earth by a simple tug of the sleeve and not a word spoken.

And when she danced away from him, it didn't matter. He stayed put, swallowed whole. Now he knew he was in costume, too, just like her -- dressed as himself at last.

First line by Kate Nies Brigham

Limitless Time

A priest, an Irishman, a cow, and a tire iron walked into a bar. They were all the same person, you see, and none of the descriptions really captured the man behind this myth. I said he's a priest because he *Jesus Christs* a lot. I called him an Irishman because he drinks a pint of whiskey every day and by the end, he's always tripping over his tongue in an accent that he didn't have at the day's start. I teased that he's a cow because he's *utterly* unbelievable. And a tire iron? Well, he once helped me out of a jam, let's say. Who he really was doesn't matter for him any more than it mattered to you or me or the next guy over on the bus. I was on the bus. I could say such things. I looked around and I didn't see a soul here that was worth that much. I included myself in that lot, don't start thinking I have a superior attitude about myself. Once Rocco accused me of being self-important and I knocked him into the next Tuesday, which, at the time, was a clean week away. Rocco was the man I started this off with. He's the riddle I was trying to tell.

Anyways, Rocco walked into a bar and it turned out to be one of those conversations we all look back on and scratch our collective heads. He's my cousin, but, more so, my friend. And when I told this story to family, they'd turn heads and spit on the ground. Friends, though, they'd pause and look me in the eye and never blink first -- they let me. It was a sign of respect. For the story, for Rocco, for me.

Rocco could tell this story himself and I imagine he sometimes does. But I tell it more, I think. I think it means more to me, what happened. Riding around on that bus, it's all I thought about, even though it has nothing to do with this bus or the people on it or the direction we're headed.

Here's what happened. Rocco, the Irishman priest with the soul of a cow and the intention of a tire iron, walked into a bar on a sunny Sunday afternoon in some springy-warm month. He was wearing a work shirt from the mechanic's shop he ran -- a blue and white pinstriped ordeal with *Rocco* stitched in red over left side of his chest -- and he was going to the bar because his ex-wife Sally wanted him to come and sign some papers about their son Ralphie. Leave it to Sally to pick a bar on a Sunday for a meeting place about their child, right? Leave it to her. She always revved my engines, truth be told, but Rocco thought she wasn't worth too much. He loved his son, though, so he always did whatever was right by him. So, anyway, he was going to the bar for that reason but what he found instead was me, sitting at the bar, pure happenstance. I was usually alone and was so that afternoon. We each drank a pint in silence, staring at a baseball game on the TV. We never said too much. Sally showed up at some point and tried -- pretty unsuccessfully -- to aggravate Rocco into an argument and, after he signed what she wanted, she left. I said to him then, "Rocco, why did you and Sally not make it?" which maybe was a silly question since he clearly didn't like her much, but you know what he said to me? He said, "Jimmy, she laughed just like Ma," and I thought about it for a minute. He was right. Sally *did* laughed just like Ma -- our grandmother. She'd been dead a long time, since we were kids, but she had this infectious laugh that even just us talking about it would explode us youngsters into fits of giggles. Sally, she had that. How had I never noticed? So I said, "You mean you got sad when she laughed because you miss Ma?" and Rocco said, "No, Jimmy, I would hear Sally laugh and it would remind me that the only thing I liked about her was that and it made me hate her, made me hate that she had a piece of Ma in her that didn't belong to her and it wasn't fair." I said, "But you know that isn't Sally's fault, right?" and he said, "Sure, I *know* that. But what I *hear* is a dead woman projecting her voice through someone who just isn't worthy." I looked at Rocco and knew he meant it. He sipped his beer and stared at the televised baseball game. I said, "What will you do when you realize that your son has the same laugh?" Because, now that I thought about it, he did. Rocco never took his eyes off the television. He said, "My son has Ma's eyes, too. I think she blessed him that way. I think she found me a woman who could help her be reincarnate. I think he'll grow up to be the man with her laugh."

And you know what? I think Rocco is right. Every time I look at that boy now, all I can think is -- he's the newly born of the once buried. Maybe that's some kind of mumbo jumbo to you, but to me, it's relief that life comes again full circle -- that when we all die, we have the chance to come back. Rocco didn't need anyone to teach him that, but I did. I needed Rocco to teach me. All Rocco had to do was take one look at that boy and he was renewed.

I rode around on this bus and I didn't think I was anybody special. I don't think anyone was. But I did think we had limitless time to prove otherwise.

First line by Sean OhEigeartaigh

It's Probably a Hoax

It wasn't until halfway through his coffee that he noticed there was a "disintegrate" button on his keyboard, and it wasn't until just after lunch that he decided to find out what it did. His finger hovered above it for three full seconds before his co-worker Carl noticed what was happening.

"Don't become a cautionary tale, Albert," Carl tsk'd, leaning casually against the walls of his cube.

He looked up at Carl with a mixture of relief and annoyance. "It's probably a hoax."

Carl shrugged. "I don't know, man."

Albert looked back at the key. It looked innocent enough. "Do you have one on your keyboard?"

Carl nodded. "Everyone does. You've never noticed it before?"

"My system just got upgraded," Albert murmured. "How long have you had this keyboard?"

Carl's eyes rolled up in his head as he consulted some kind of internal calendar. "Few weeks."

"Am I the last one for the upgrade?" Albert asked.

"What do I look like -- the IT guy?" Carl scoffed. "How would I know?"

Albert fought back the urge to say, *"You look like the office gossip you effeminate prick"* and instead swiveled his chair back around to stare at the keyboard. "No one else has pushed this key?" he marveled.

Carl leaned in and dropped his voice. "Lisa did," he whispered.

Albert's features scrunched up. "Which one is that?" he asked.

"Super hot, big rack, blonde with big daddy's girl blue eyes," Carl spouted, his voice back to a regular decibel. "Kinda dumb, maybe? Actually, who knows, I never listened to her when she spoke to me."

Albert frowned. "Don't know who she is."

Carl rolled his eyes. "The hottest bitch in this drab, pathetic wasteland? You don't notice her?"

"I guess I don't notice *bitches*," Albert muttered, grinding his teeth.

"Well, your loss, friend. Anyway, she pushed the button, maybe by accident. She was trying to hit *shift* and then the hastag for some tweet she was sending -- ironically about the self-destruct button --"

"Disintegrate," Albert corrected.

"Whatever," Carl said. "The point is, she hit it and... No more Lisa."

"She got in trouble?" Albert queried.

"No, dumbass. *She disappeared,*" Carl reported.

Albert laughed. "What?"

"No shit, man! The button made *her* disintegrate. Or combust. Or something. Anyway, no one's seen her since. Maybe you *did* know who she was but she's been erased from your memory or something because of the button," Carl mused.

Albert stared at Carl and tried to weigh the bullshit factor into what he was hearing. Carl stared at him, expressionless. So Albert got up and breezed past Carl to Sofia's cube a few down from his own.

"Did you know Lisa?" he asked.

Sofia blinked at him. "Who?"

"Lisa. Blonde." Albert ran out of adjectives that he felt were appropriate to repeat from Carl's description.

Sofia kept blinking. "Um... No?"

Carl chuckled. "She must've been erased from your recollection as well!"

"What?" Sofia asked.

Carl guided Albert away from their confused co-worker. "See? It's dangerous stuff," he said.

"So why do you remember her?" Albert asked.

Carl shrugged. "I fucked her once, so maybe because I knew her outside of the office..."

Albert became extra dubious. "You said she was hot?"

"Smokin'," Carl confirmed.

"Hot women don't sleep with you," Albert said.

"This one did," Carl confirmed, making what can only be described as an obscene gesture.

"OK, that's how I know you're lying. You made her up. You probably even planted this fake keyboard here with the extra key to prank me," Albert said, sitting back in his chair with utter confidence.

Carl ran his fingers through his hair. "That's crazy," he said.

"That's you," Albert said, plunging his pointer finger onto the "disintegrate" key.

And then the world went black in a quick, tiny pop.

First line by Rob Rogers

The Stranger of Love

He must have come from over there on a gust of wind. Sitting in front of me, he had a careless look about him, as if he could be so easily tossed about by a moderate force of nature. I considered myself a moderate force of nature, so it's with a scrutinizing eye that I took him in. Somewhere my friend Mally was laughing uncontrollably at how fussy I was being, even then. Even when I knew this was the real deal -- this was an act of God.

"I don't know," he said suddenly and I cocked my head towards him.

"Don't know what?" I asked.

"I don't know the answer," he said with a shine in his eye that reflected the devil in his core.

"The answer is *always*," I said as I got up from my seat and walked away from him and left it up to him if he'd like to follow or not. I knew he'd follow. He'd always follow.

A few short weeks ago, Mally and I sat drinking vodka-soaked vanilla milkshakes we'd made in my apartment at four in the morning and struggled with the mystery of men. She was recently single after a seven-year hostage crisis finally ended with her walking freely out the door. I was single, but in the forever sort of way. I liked casual affairs that left me remembering the essence of the man instead of his entire being and to hell with his full name. I referred to them by nicknames like Flatty and Seven Pack and Juan Two and I believed, unlike the romantic Mally, that love was a myth ready to be busted. I was certain no man had ever loved me, at least, and when I'd tried to extend myself to try it out, it had ended in utter destruction. I'd had men leave their wives over me only to cast me aside moments later with little more than an upturned glance. To say I was *jaded* was an understatement. And in that lost, dark hour, Mally was like me -- bitter and hardened by the burden of the unrequited.

"*Trying* doesn't even matter," she was saying. "*Trying* is for little leaguers. When you *try* as an adult, you've already failed."

My eyes were a little red from the all-nighter we were pulling. I sniffed a bit and added, "Failure is always an option, even though they say it's not."

Mally lolled her gaze towards me and said, "I really though Skinny Jeans liked you, too."

I shrugged. "You think they all like me."

"Yes, but this guy -- this guy showed up at your recital and he hates classical music and he bought you dinner that night even though we were all gathered around the table with you and he hung on your every word." Mally paused and stared into her milkshake. "Men are such simple creatures. How could this turn out wrong?"

"How could Jay cheat on you?" I quipped. "After everything you did for him -- supporting him when he lost his job and being there while his sister went through chemo. How could he turn on you?"

Mally's eyes darkened. "You never liked him. Don't make this about Jay."
I shrugged. "I never liked him, but that doesn't make the way he treated you any less shitty."

"No, it proves your point, a point you tried to make for seven years. He didn't love me."

"He didn't love you *the right way*," I corrected. "He loved you, though. He's just a pathetic specimen."

"They're all pathetic specimens," she muttered.

I grinned despite myself and the late hour. "Welcome to the dark side," I said.

Two short days later, I was walking along the pier towards my father's boat when a man fell in step with me. It was dusk and the docks could be unsettling in the dark, but I wasn't afraid. The man had his hands shoved deep in the pockets of some faded jeans, his red plaid shirt unbuttoned with a navy t-shirt underneath. His hair was a wild mess of brown curls and when he spoke, his voice had a distinct authority to it that immediately slowed my steps.

"I never do this," he said.

I turned, tossing my long blonde hair across my opposite shoulder. "Do what?"

"This," he said, reaching over and taking hold of my hand.

It was sharp, magnetic, relentless. I felt awake for the first time in my life. It made me stop moving and turn to face him. His eyes were a dark green and he smiled with only half of his mouth. I chewed the inside of my lip and stared at him, eyes narrowed.

"In some cultures, this would constitute first base," I said coyly, raising our linked hands in the air.

His half smile brightened. "In some cultures, this would constitute marriage. I'm Sam," he said, squeezing my hand.

"Annmarie," I said.

We stood with linked hands for an awkwardly long time without speaking and then he leaned over and kissed me on the cheek.

"Let's go to dinner," he said.

"OK," I said without thinking.

That was the last moment Sam was in charge of our destiny. After that, I steered the ship, deciding what restaurant we should dine at, where we should have cocktails after our meal, and whose bed we would sleep in that night. We didn't have sex that first night -- we just lay in my bed with only our feet touching as we drifted off to sleep. And when my father asked me the next day why I hadn't come to the boat, I had told him the truth -- "I was with Sam" -- as if *Sam* were a longstanding member of our extended family and my father had paused and said, "Oh," and questioned me no further.

Sam and I were inseparable because I preferred it that way, a realization that flattened me. I had never wanted to spend this much time with any human being and yet here was this perfect stranger who had possessed me, body and soul. He would say to me, "Annmarie, I will always be right where you need me" and I believed him. There was a sense of forever pressed into our combined sensibility and it didn't scare me like it should -- it thrilled me. I *owned* him. He *belonged* to me. Finally. I was opening my eyes to a new wave of love -- because truthfully, he owned me, too. I was possessed.

My inner skeptic kept quiet but alert as I looked for a reason to doubt what I believed to be true and I chose not to tell Mally or anyone beyond my questioning father about this rumble of romance in my life because I was sure, at any moment, it would be snatched away like so many before. I even thought of what nickname I'd dub Sam when he cut and run but I could think of none.

And on that day, as I stood and walked away, Sam did follow and he followed and he followed until all that was left was a long path of footprints that carried me forward.

First line by Shannon Robinson

Unity of the Space

As she settled into *savasana*, the feeling only grew stronger and she instinctively wrapped her fingers around the stranger's hand next to her. It was peace. It was love. It was an intense swirl of calm and knowing. The stranger seemed to feel it, too -- he squeezed her fingers and she felt something overwhelming fill her gut. Trailed by the scent of mint, their teacher moved administering final grounding adjustments. The practice had been fluid and strong, empowering. She had never practiced at this studio before, but something had drawn her in this evening, to this teacher, to this spot on the floor beside a stranger whose practice was both humble and admirable. It was a new style for her, but he seemed at home in this heated space, flowing through Sun Salutations and Warrior variations. He seemed accustomed to this teacher and the commanding voice projected from her tiny body which moved with grace around the room, demonstrating almost nothing physically, allowing her verbal cues to set the pace and the tone. As a new student, she had let this stranger beside her serve as the role model for what the teacher's voice instructed. And now as their practice symbolically died in this final resting posture, she knew her fingers intertwining with his was the most appropriate form of thank you she could administer. This was a practice that taught stillness of mind, humbleness of purpose, and gratitude for the present moment, all things that she valued but hadn't quite understood how to enact until she rolled out her mat and pressed her bare feet into the soft rubber -- and hadn't understood until she'd found herself beside such a kindred spirit of kindness who housed intoxicating levels of grace that she could breath in and exhale as recycled goodness bound with her own. This was her ideal moment. This was her ideal space. This was a time to replay forever. Soon the teacher would rouse them from their rest, call for their hands and feet to regain motion, to push out a final cleansing breath before curling up and rocking over to press their foreheads against the floor as a means of sealing in this new energy they'd cultivated before sitting quietly, upright, for a final few moments before bowing out a heartfelt *namaste*. By then, she and the stranger would have let go of each other -- but that time had not come yet. With their fingers curled together, she felt his heartbeat through her own veins and it warmed her and it made the unity of the space wrap around her in such a way that she knew, finally, what true happiness was, and it was a feeling she'd carry with her forever, no matter what happened next.

First line by Anne Nolan

Like a Rainbow in the Dark

"We're a lie, you and I.
We're words without a rhyme."

~ *Dio*

Christmas morning yawned awake, groggy and pale with a lulling fog that would have ordinarily made Grace feel nostalgic and drawn to the romanticism of this singular moment, but hearing her husband Charles in the bathroom spitting toothpaste in the sink made her entire being clench. Somewhere down the hall, her two children Anthony and Olivia were giggling their way awake, ready to see Santa's late night delivery under their Christmas tree. Grace drew the blankets up under her chin and closed her eyes as she heard the bathroom door open and Charles sigh his way back into the room.

"Grace, I'm going to start breakfast, OK?"

She tightened the close of her eyes. "Sure," she said.

Her mind flicked back to the night before when they made a brave united front and brought their children to the Children's Mass and then over to a friends' for cider and donuts, a Christmas Eve tradition the families in the neighborhood had started when their children started being old enough to toddle around and chant *Ho, ho, ho!* All night long, she wore a broad smile and wondered if it was as transparent as it felt. She eyed her husband wearing a similar strain across the room and her heart sank, knowing that even if she was being convincing, he was not. But if anyone saw the tension, they left it alone, opting to hoist glasses in cheers and sneak their friends' children candy canes and snowman-shaped sugar cookies. The only sign of anyone picking up on a thing was seven-year-old Olivia who murmured, "You'll be happier once you see what Santa brings you, Mama," as she was tucked into bed.

With the covers still drawn up to her chin, Grace opened her eyes and stared at the large red digits on her alarm clock. 8:15AM. She forced herself to exhale deeply, releasing some of the rigidity in her body, and she sat up. Down the hall, she could hear Anthony yelling, "I smell bacon!" and the sound of two small sets of feet pounding their way towards the stairs. Grace smiled at that and followed her children's lead, allowing herself several moments to inhale and exhale the heavenly aroma of breakfast. *Ahh.* There were so many little joys to appreciate.

Sliding out of bed, Grace shrugged on her Boston University hooded sweatshirt and a pair of once-bright-and-fluffy red slippers and scooted in the direction of her gleeful offspring, who had been distracted in their pursuit of bacon by the piles of brightly wrapped gifts under their perfectly shaped tree. Grace leaned in the doorway and smiled again, thinking of the day they'd lugged that tree into the house, only fifteen days prior, and after the initial flush of cheeks settled and the tree was upright in its holder, skirt intact, and the boxes of lights and ornaments wrestled from the crawl space in the attic, the afternoon had been quite pleasant -- just Grace, Charles, Anthony, and Olivia with their two cats Springy and Elmo weaving between their feet and batting at the low hung treasures as Christmas classics played on the radio.

"Look, pretty, rainbow!" Olivia had cooed as one of her favorite glass angel ornaments splintered the light from tree onto the white skirt on the floor.

Charles had wrapped Grace in his arms and held her warmly against his body as they leaned their heads together and silently enjoyed the bickering back and forth between their five- and seven-year-old children, little humans so much like themselves it often made them shiver. They'd been so happy that day -- so sure about their place in this time and confident about the future bearing similar fruits. The unshakable family tree: they were rooted and climbing all at the same time.

Grace jumped back into the present when Charles was suddenly at her shoulder with a mug of coffee in his hand.

"I added some Bailey's," he said as he handed it to her.

"Thanks," she said, the warmth of her remembering being replaced by the chill of the moment.

"Mama! Look at all the toys from Santa!" Anthony yelled, flapping his hands in the air as he hovered near the pile.

"Well, let's see what he brought you," Grace said, easing away from her husband to sit on the floor between her children.

Charles also came to sit on the floor, though he leaned against the couch instead of crouching in their cluster. Grace could feel his eyes on the back of her head and it made her jaw clench. Her mind triggered back to that night they'd assembled the Christmas tree, after the children were tucked into bed and she'd sat in this very spot with her husband beside her as they stared at the Olivia's rainbow angel. Grace'd kissed him and felt the strength of love, family, and the unity that created flow through her. With her chin resting on his shoulder, she'd smiled lazily at this man she'd cherished for a decade of marriage and said, "When I put Liv to bed tonight, she asked me if that rainbow would still be there, even over night. She's such a sweet girl."

"What did you tell her?" Charles asked, tucking his chin in towards his chest.

Something in his body language made Grace pull back as her eyes swept over him. "I told her the darkness might make it hard to see a rainbow."

"Hmm," Charles sighed.

"Is something wrong?" Grace asked.

Charles lifted his head from his chest and looked her square the in eye. "You'll want a divorce," he said.

Grace felt her heart jump into her throat. "What?" she asked.

"After I tell you," he said, his eyes sad and heavy. "I'm so sorry, Grace."

"Sorry for what?" she asked. "You're scaring me."

Charles drew in a tight breath and pulled his knees into his chest. "I had an affair," he said softly. "I've been having an affair."

"What?" Grace rasped.

"She's pregnant," Charles went on, his gaze dropping back to the floor. "She's pregnant and I made her get a DNA test and it conclusively proves that I am the baby's father."

Grace felt her entire body turn into liquid. "What?" she repeated.

"We just got the test results," Charles said, his eyes flicking back towards his wife.

"When?" Grace asked, desperate to form other words besides *what*.

"Yesterday," Charles said. "I didn't want to ruin our Christmas tree day."

Grace realized hot tears were rolling down her cheeks and she wiped them away with a hard hand against her cheek. "Well, you did a shitty job at that," she said.

"I mean, for the kids," Charles said. "I didn't want to ruin it for them."

"Oh," Grace said in a hollow voice. "I see."

"I'm so sorry," Charles said again. "I was stupid and careless..."

"Who is she?" Grace asked, her tone turning angry.

"Ruth," Charles said, his shoulders slumping.

"Ruth Piel?" Grace asked.

Charles hung his head. "Grace, I never meant..."

"When did you start fucking her?" Grace demanded.

"Grace, I..." Charles began.

She held up her hand. "It doesn't matter," she said. "You got your old news ex-girlfriend pregnant. And you clearly didn't take proper precautions so now I probably need to go in for an STD screening." She made herself stop talking and she stared at him. "How could you?"

Charles covered his face with his hand. "I have nothing to say in my defense. But I needed to let you know as soon as possible so you could tell me what you want to do."

Grace jumped to her feet and stalked away from him. "Of course it's up to me," she said. "You fuck up and I'm the one who has to make all the decisions about how we handle it as a family. You're a coward."

Charles never came up to bed that night while Grace tossed and turned and let conspiracy theories run rampant through her brain. At one point, she even became convinced that he'd left to go and be with Ruth, which enraged her so much, she flew out of bed and went to make sure he was still in the house. He was -- sleeping on the couch. But even *that* enraged her -- how could he be sleeping at all? Her pain was unbearable. But when the morning came around, she put her *Mom* face on and powered through getting her kids up and ready for school, a task made easier because Charles had left for work, presumably, early that day. All day, she wondered if he'd come home or not and she couldn't decide which result she wanted.

And all day she stewed in silence, wanting to tell someone, anyone, what had happened but she couldn't put the words together coherently and she didn't know what she wanted to do about her marriage and her family and her husband's illegitimate child growing cell by cell in the uterus of the woman from whom Grace had once stolen the love of her life. Was this karma? Was this due process? Grace thought back to the early days when she and Charles had met volunteering at an autism telethon, a cause they both held dear to their hearts because they had family members who lived with the disability, and they'd ended up wrapped in conversation long after the lights were out on their day and Grace had felt electrified by this eloquent man with a sensitive heart. Even finding out he had a girlfriend with whom he lived didn't deter her from wanting what wasn't yet hers. She made it her mission to drive a wedge between Charles and Ruth, a woman she found to be kind but naive, and by the time Grace succeeded in getting what she wanted, Ruth was left dumbfounded on the sidewalk with a box full of her belongings at her feet. Grace hadn't thought of her in years -- she didn't even know the woman was still around. And now her entire life was being overturned by a simple plus sign.

Charles did return back home after work that evening and he'd helped Anthony put together a train set under the tree while Grace helped Olivia with her homework in the other room. After the kids were in bed, Grace had drawn Charles into their bedroom and whispered in a desperate voice, "Just sleep here tonight." Charles had looked surprised, but he complied, the two of them spooned together in heart pounding uncertainty. "I didn't think you'd want me here," he'd murmured into her ear. Even feeling his intimate breath against her skin made her slightly nauseous, but she held firm to her conviction that she needed him in their bed with her and didn't respond in any way beside squeezing his forearm draped across her chest.

The next night, she found herself craving an even deeper intimacy with him, so she once again invited him into their bed -- and into her body. They made love like they hadn't since their early days when the intensity of their honeymoon faze rocked them almost violently. She was surprised that feeling his lips against hers, his skin against her skin, didn't repulse her. She was a woman who was desperate to hang onto the idyllic life she'd taken for granted until two nights prior and he was eager to comply with all of her wishes.

"You surprise me, Grace," Charles said as he laid back on his pillow.

Grace had turned to face his profile and had a sudden violent urge to hurt him physically somehow -- an urge that she quieted and left undone. Instead, she bit her lip hard and hoped she didn't draw any of her own blood.

After that night, they spent every consecutive night in a similar fashion with Grace's mind running wild with dreams of triumphantly announcing her own new baby on the way and the look on Ruth's face when she found out she still hadn't won -- that Grace would always win. But then in the morning, she'd look at Anthony and Olivia and she'd feel a horrible wave of guilt that she'd even *dream* of bringing a new life into the world for such spiteful reasons. When her period started the day before Christmas, she'd actually felt a dumb gust of relief and before she and Charles took the children to church that evening, she pulled him aside and said, "We'll need to have a serious discussion after the holiday." Charles' face lost its consistent look of tentative hopefulness as he'd nodded in agreement. "Of course," he said.

Now that Christmas morning was here, though, Grace felt sick as she watched her children throw their arms around their father and then circle back to her as they cried out thanks for a prized Christmas morning, complete with crackled bacon. Grace couldn't help but wonder what Ruth was doing right then and if her husband had called her to find out. With her heart heavy, she stayed by herself an extra few minutes by the tree while the rest of her family moved to the kitchen for breakfast. Her eyes settled resolutely on the glass angel and the rainbow it produced and then her lids slide closed, a test to see if the fractured light still remained.

Story inspired by Dio's "Like a Rainbow in the Dark" (via Dave Fertig)

I'll Tell You Why

So me and Lois are driving up to Vermont to get an abortion. I know your first question -- why Vermont? I'll tell you why. Lois is a goddamn sucker for leaf peeping. She says to me, "Benny, can't we just drive to Vermont and enjoy the show nature intended for us?" She's my Lois, I can deny her nothing, so I said, "Sure, baby. We'll just find a clinic as far north in Vermont as we can so that we can enjoy the leaves and then take care of business." You'd think I'd hung the friggin moon the way she *Oh, Benny*'d me for that slice of brain power. Anyway, we left Arlington, Mass and started driving on this fine Tuesday morning in October and I couldn't think of a better time in my life. Maybe you want to know why Tuesday. Easy -- no traffic. Regular folk were all working their sad lives away today. But not me and Lois, oh no. We're on our way to Vermont. We've had classic rock blaring on the radio and the windows rolled down and she had her aviators on and I had my Sox hat and what else could we need in this life? This woman, she made me so happy. And she was so right about the leaves. God, I'd never seen anything more spectacular in my life! It took this woman from Alabama to show this New England guy all about the wonder of the region. Go figure. I'd never leaf peeped in my life but as we drove along, I thought to myself, *I can't wait to do this every year from now on, me and Lois, jeepers-peepers.*

"Hey, baby, how about us calling ourselves Jeepers-Peepers on this roadtrip?" I said.

She grinned at me from behind those aviators, her round happy cheeks convulsing with giggles. "You mean like when we check in?" she asked.

I hadn't actually thought of that, but I liked where her brain was headed. "Sure, baby, why not?"

"Why not?" she echoed as she stuck her hand out the window to feel it cut through the air.

Every twenty miles or so, we'd stop the car and get out to stretch our legs and look around. Everything was quiet but brimming with autumnal life. Fuck yeah I said "autumnal life." Just because I have this stupid Boston accent don't mean I'm an idiot. I went to Tufts, for chrissakes, and I read Shakespeare AND liked it. So, yeah, I got some vocabulary that might surprise you. Tufts is also where I met my Lois. We took a geography class together -- *world* geography. Man, if you ever wanna feel like an ignorant fuck, take a world geography class. Take me out of North America and I'm a friggin fish outta water. I didn't know Hong Kong was a country -- I thought it was a city, all this time! But maybe it is? Even after taking that godforsaken class, I sure as shit don't know. Lois, though, she was pretty decent at it. She'd been to Africa, even. A girl from Alabama who went to Africa on a *high school trip*. Where did Lois come from? I tell you, I am constantly reminded how lucky I am to be with such a treasure. And she helped me make it through that world geography class -- that was her first unofficial assignment.

We always joked, see, about *unofficial assignments*. Like, if Lois didn't know the Sox starting line up or which seven beers were always on tap at Foster's, it's my unofficial assignment to teach her. And with me -- if I didn't know what celebrities were getting divorced or what movie was #1 at the box office over the weekend, she'd let me know. This leaf peeping adventure also counted as an unofficial assignment. It's like the shit we know that our better half didn't know but we'd like them to know because it's important and since we already knew it, we could graciously teach it to each other. Get it?

Holy shit, I loved this woman. And she loved me. That's sort of the bottom line here, folks.

We made it through New Hampshire, stopping to have lunch at a coffee shop in Grantham along the way, and as we crossed the border into Vermont, Lois reached over and squeezed my hand. Her other hand rested on her lower abdomen and she didn't say a word, but I could feel it in her fingers -- she was nervous, excited, and committed -- I felt the same way. I responded by squeezing back and not letting go first. She could let go when she needed to, that was going to be her decision. I think she hung on for a pretty long time because my hand started to get a little numb, but I didn't care. I would do anything for this woman. She was my everything.

We still stopped every once in awhile in Vermont to breath in the air and feel the force of nature around us. Some people enjoy hiking and being outdoors like this and I never thought I was one of them, but maybe this trip was going to reveal a whole new side of me to me. I guess it already was. All I had to do was look over at Lois and see her radiating with light -- god, I wish you could have seen her. Her goodness was just that vibrant, her love that strong. I wondered if I glowed like she did -- I felt like it was a pretty sure thing that I did. Especially when we touched any part of our bodies together, even just finger tips. I felt like I was exploding around this woman -- like a firecracker -- like a crack of lightening. I hope you know what this kind of love feels like -- I sincerely do. I never did until I met Lois and standing beside her, looking out at the nature in Vermont, I inhaled and exhaled pure bliss.

We didn't talk much, though, once we were in Vermont. What do we really have to say after all this time together? We'd been out of Tufts for two years now and we lived together as caretakers for my grandmother's house in Arlington, so we spent a lot of time together, quiet time, with not many other people around. I'd learned that you can say so many things in the quiet -- that so many things did not require the use of your voice. Who *knew* that? Lois, man, she taught me everything, even when she wasn't saying a word.

It wasn't until we were about a mile away from the clinic and an hour away from her scheduled appointment that Lois spoke up again. And when she did, she said, "Benny, I couldn't love you more."

I grinned at her and said, "Baby, I love you, too."

And when we got to the clinic, we walked in hand-in-hand and did what we'd come to do -- love, support, and fulfill each other in the best way we possibly could.

First line by Tim Langan

More Easily Broken

Every once in awhile, I wonder if anyone else gauges how good of a night they had by what their knuckles look like in the morning. This morning, my knuckles are bruised but not bandaged. I sit at the bus stop and stare at them with great interest. Have you ever really taken the time to do what I'm doing right now? Have you ever stopped and really examined all of the millions of pieces that come together to make *you*? It makes so much sense to read palms -- your body knows your story -- it builds itself just for you -- it provides the vessel for you to live the life you're intended to live. Do you ever even pause to consider that? Well, I do. Every day.

Like now. At this bus stop. It's cold this morning, cold for September. I've got on my work boots and some jeans and a baggy sweatshirt with a Budweiser logo on it. I don't even drink anymore. Or work, really, for that matter. I glance away from the repeating patterns in the flesh on my knuckles and consider the only other person waiting for the bus. She's young, probably a college student, and she's not dressed for the cold. Flip flops, really? She's not facing me but she is standing with her arms wrapped intensely around her body as she bops back and forth from one foot to the other. Her hair is swept back in a long brown ponytail and her bright blue messenger bag appears a little too full. Just from her body language, I construct her life story: suburban girl, pleasant life (but not *too* pleasant -- she is waiting for a bus, after all), moved here to the big city for college because her parents wanted her to go to one of their alma maters and have the "city experience," and now here she is, unprepared for unseasonable cold. I shake my head slowly. Parents think they can prepare their children for everything, but they can't. Sometimes their college-age daughter still wears flip flips when it's only 42 degrees. I'm sure her skin is ripe with goose bumps.

I tuck my gaze back in towards my knuckles and take a moment to admire the scars on the back of my left hand. For some reason, I only have scars on that hand, not the right. I read somewhere once that our dominant side healed faster than our less dominant side, but that only sort of explained why my right side would be immune from permanent damage. I like my scars, though. They were another way I gauged my happiness. I like how they interrupt the natural progression of the lines on my hand. I like how they discolor my otherwise standard white skin. I like how if I lean in close enough, I can hear their stories and I can relive their birth. None of the scars were new. These, these were all old friends and I admired each and every one of them. It had been awhile since I'd added a new one, actually. Funny. There was a time when my flesh was less disciplined, I guess. A time when I was more easily broken.

That time has passed.

The girl sharing the bus stop with me suddenly sneezes with what seems like her entire body and digs desperately in her bag for a tissue, I presume, before finally giving up and wiping her nose on her sleeve. I am marveled at her -- how will she ever make it? What will she learn from this grave morning waiting for the bus? I stare back at my knuckles and smile and don't think about my future beyond this single moment. If I wanted to know about that kind of thing, I'd flip my hand over and read my palm instead.

First line by Josh "Ja-key" Hurd

The Yoga of Chocolate Cake

Chocolate cake references aside, *moist* is undeniably one of the least appealing words in the English language. I feel moist right now -- I am unappealing. Exiting the hot yoga studio, I grab my bag and slide my feet into flip flops and push my way outside. It's a refreshing sixty-five degrees and sunny. I stop for a moment and smile with my eyes closed, sweeping my arms up over my head one final time in yoga-mode. Opening my eyes back up, I turn my attention down the road and head home. A shower is in order. I have a chocolate cake to bake.

My roommates both work a typical 9-5 so they're not around at four in the afternoon. It's unbelievably wonderful to walk into that small, cluttered space and not feel crowded. I enter my room and take a moment to scrutinize myself in my full length mirror. I stand in *tadasana*, mountain pose, feet together, back straight, hands flared out from the side of my body. My long black hair is swept back in a messy pony tail and jagged sweat streaks are still soaked into my clothing. I don't know how long I stand there like this, just staring at me -- in this moment -- Mountain Girl. Am I fierce and stable? Am I simultaneously at my peak and at my base? What does it mean to stand here like this?

I have a long way to go.

Releasing the pose, I pull my tank top over my head in one swift movement and hurl it towards my closet door. Later, I'll throw it in the laundry basket. But for the moment, I'm all about efficiency. Leaving my yoga pants and sports bra on, I exit my room and I head for the shower. I turn on the water and, when it's just right, I step into the flow and hum an unfamiliar tune. I am coming down from *moist* and through this cleansing-by-water, I am reborn fresh. By the time I step out of the shower, I am happy and wrapped in a bright yellow towel. Padding down the hall to my room, I leave the towel on my floor for a little while, walking around the room a tad aimless and naked. Moments like this remind me of childhood, of freedom, of joy. But moments are all that

I will allow before I snap back into focus. I dress quickly in a pair of blue jeans and plain blue long sleeve t-shirt. Leaving my hair damp and hanging down my back, I slide my feet into some slippers and make my way into the kitchen. I glance at the clock and figure that I have at least two hours before the first roommate will return home. Perfect.

I assemble all of the necessary ingredients -- eggs, butter, cocoa, flour... -- and I begin to mix from memory. My mother taught me this recipe when I was a very small child and together she and I perfected it over our shared lifetime. I could make this cake blindfolded. I can tell how good a batter is just by stirring it. This one that I'm making today, this one is going to be rich and delicious.

I work in quiet today. Usually, I turn on some music or get a friend on speaker phone, but today I am a mountain -- I am stoic and majestic. I am more interested in what will make this cake please the man I'm making it for. He's heard so many things about my skills in this area and since he's experienced my skills in so many others, I thought it might be nice to let him in on this slice of me that so many have sampled before. As I pour the batter into the cake pan, I watch its rich flow and smile. I take the tip of my finger and I draw a heart into the center. It'll bake away, but I am pleased with its temporary inclusion.

Once it's in the oven, I slip back into my room and sprawl on my bed, my eyes towards the ceiling. I am comfortable and clean and happy. Everything about this afternoon is so pleasant. Even my moistness before was lovely -- it proved I had worked hard in class and done my practice justice. And, mostly, it was easily remedied. I lay still on my bed while the cake bakes. My hair dries and adopts a slight wave. I run my hands through it to feel how uneven it is while at the same time feeling silky and cool. Maybe I drift off to sleep for a short time. Maybe I just suspend the acknowledgement of time. Maybe time is something arbitrary and immeasurable. Maybe lying there so still is my day's equivalent of fun. No matter the case, the timer rings and I return to my creation, withdrawing it from the oven. I examine it hypercritically and decide it passes my inspection. As I set it aside to cool, I begin to make a chocolate ganache frosting that aims to please. Here I use Martha Stewart's recipe because it's better than anything I've tried to create on my own. I usually make a butter cream, but my intended audience hinted at a preference for the other, so I am willing to be accommodating. Everything smells like chocolate and heaven. I close my eyes as I stir the frosting by hand until its consistency is perfect. The cake is still cooling, of course, so I follow Martha's instructions and leave my frosting in the refrigerator, stirring it every five minutes or so, until the cake seems cool enough. And then I frost with even strokes of the spatula. This reminds me of the definition of *vinyasa -- to place carefully* or *to move with the breath*. That is exactly what I have done here.

As if he'd been waiting for this exact moment, this is when he calls me. I inhale the chocolate-y aroma and exhale out a sigh of relief for this good timing. I tell him I will be ready for him when he gets here. I do not tell him there will be moist cake involved.

First line by Jennie Siegel

The Haggis

It was my first experience with haggis. I was in Scotland just for a weekend with my oldest friends Abaleen and Joseph and we were having a miserable time. Joseph had made the trip with a purpose -- work related -- while Abaleen and I had merely tagged along, as we often did. Why Joseph put up with us, I have no idea. We were rowdy and careless and inconsiderate, especially in all matters related to him. Abaleen and I never talked about it, but I think it's because we both secretly were head-over-heels in love with him but we knew neither of us could claim him as our own. Instead, we spent our time trying to make ourselves as spiteful and unappealing as humanly possible. It must have worked because he never even so much as tried to kiss either one of us, not even when we all crowded into the same bed in his hotel room this trip. "Dora, move over," was all he murmured into my ear.

It rained our entire stay in Glasgow and unpleasantly so. We lived just outside Raleigh, North Carolina so we were used to rain that we cutely coined "vacation rain." The sort that tourists maybe didn't mind so much because it was frilly and romantic. The rain in Scotland was punishing and relentless. Abaleen and I refused to buy umbrellas and we walked the city in raincoats we'd brought from home. We also fought the entire time in the way that sisters do: cutting because it's all true. On our last full day, we stumbled into a hole-in-the-wall bar near our hotel where we ordered our usual fair -- cheap beer and expensive Scotch. We had learned on this trip that *Scotch* is actually whiskey and this tidbit delighted us. We learned how to order it properly -- neat, two fingers -- and we drank it with gusto that seemed to amuse the old men in the bars. We had also learned that the only way we'd understand a damn thing any of them was saying was if we had a few drinks first, so we made a point of drinking early and often. Every time, we toasted Joseph, who had loaned us the money for all of this partying. We didn't have money -- or jobs, for that matter. We appreciated his corporate sponsorship.

Is this bar, the last one we'd spend time in on this trip abroad as it would turn out, we made easy friends with the bartender, older than Macbeth and harry as all get out. He was the easiest person in the country to understand, though, because he was hard of hearing and worked by writing notes in a little pocket sized notepad. We borrowed some paper from him and jotted down little *life goals* to pass the time while we waited for Joseph to come and meet us.

"Tomorrow, I will balance on my nose," I read aloud.

"Tomorrow, I will read *Moby Dick*," Abaleen read aloud. She winked at me. "Both impossible," she added as we each slipped our yellow pieces of paper into our wallets. Abaleen was big on what she called *mañana promises* -- something that will never happen but, well, maybe it will!

I slid the notepad back across the bar so our new friend could do his job effectively, although we soon realized that everyone else there communicated with him by what appeared to be a standard issue sign language. The notepad was for tourists like us. Abaleen and I bought the bartender a drink and made him toast with us.

"To the written word!" I declared as we clinked our glasses together.

By the time Joseph found us, we were extremely drunk and both a little in love with our bartender, who had written his name in neat handwriting for us -- D O N A L D. Joseph sighed when he found us but ordered us another round and asked if we were hungry.

Have the haggis. Best in Scotland, Donald wrote.

"Have the haggis!" Abaleen yelped with a giggle.

Joseph grayed a little. "Do you know what haggis is, Abs?"

She shook her head and so did I. "Tell us what it is, world traveler," I said with a sloppy smile.

Joseph leaned in as if he had an awful secret. "They take a sheep's internal organs, like heart, lungs, liver, that sort of stuff, and grind it all up together and then add other stuff like onions and spices and whatever, and then simmer it all up in the sheep's stomach for like three hours."

"Sounds good, we'll take three," Abaleen said, holding up three fingers to Donald.

"Three haggis!" She hiccuped.

Joseph closed his eyes and sighed again. "Abs..." he said.

Even in my drunken state, I agreed with Joseph. Haggis sounded disgusting, like the sort of thing I'd see a wild animal eat on a nature show that would make me gag just from watching.

"It's no different than eating hotdogs," Abaleen said, her voice stiffening at our resistance. "And I've seen both of you eat hotdogs repeatedly all of your lives."

Somehow she always managed to be both convincing and succinct. "Good point, Abaleen," I conceded. I would eat the haggis. "When in Rome..." I said, nudging Joseph in the ribs.

He was clearly not drunk enough for this.

"I always thought haggis was an animal native to Scotland with legs longer on one side than the other so it could run around the hills effortlessly," Abaleen said after we'd all been quiet for a few moments.

Donald grinned at her and wrote *Tourist* on his notepad before sliding three plates in front of us. I stared at the dish before me with a mixture of curiosity and horror -- the horror mostly being the knowledge of what it was, exactly, that I was about it eat. It was a bland color, a shade I liked to call *deep fried*, and served with a side of chips. Even though Abaleen had seemed to be the most gung ho about this experience, she, too, sat with her hands folded in her lap, staring at her plate. Joseph's arms were folded across his chest. Sitting in between them, I glanced side to side and then plucked one deep fried ball off my plate and popped it into my mouth. My eyes grew wide as I chewed.

"Not bad," I said with my mouth full. I plucked another ball off my plate and shoved it into my mouth.

Donald laughed at my lack of grace but he applauded my effort. The twinkle in his eye that he'd shared with Abaleen and me now strictly belonged to me. I smiled as I wiped my mouth.

Later that night, I said I was going to use the bathroom but instead followed Donald out into the rain under the guise of *smoke break*, even though I did not, at the time, smoke. He did though, a fat cigar that he allowed me to puff on a few times before we made out a little. Back inside, I barely said a word about it but Abaleen's eyes swam all over me as if they were looking for a lifeboat. I didn't pay her any mind and instead, winked sloppily at the man back behind the bar. There was something romantic and nostalgic about him, something I never quite understood until we were back in the states and I realized that what I'd done was break the Joseph Code -- I'd taken a shared man and made him mine. Abaleen and I were never quite the same again after that, no matter how small this moment in time might seem.

Before that could happen, though, I ate everything on my plate as if it were my last meal on earth. It was my last meal in Scotland, so maybe that's exactly what it was. Abaleen and Joseph didn't touch their plates. I barely noticed.

First line by Karen Caiazzo

Dust and Damp

"The matches won't strike!" Richard yelled from the living room. We hadn't been to the cabin in months, and everything was covered in a solid layer of dust and damp. Bird sang tunelessly from outside the window, and I wondered aloud if a fire in the fireplace was absolutely the *first* thing that needed his attention when we arrived.

"How else to you expect it to seem less depressing in here?" he shot back.

I stood in the living room doorway and folded my arms across my chest. "With some lemon Pledge," I said.

The tension in his shoulders relaxed as he chuckled. "Listen, babe, you do that and I'll do this and together, we'll remind ourselves why we love this place so much."
I listened carefully to those words and tried to determine if they actually held the double meaning I inferred -- could he mean that we'd remind ourselves why we loved *each other* so much? I stared at his back and was sure that, as usual, he meant what he said and only that. I sighed and left the living room to track down that Pledge.

Half an hour later, he'd managed to get the fire blazing and I'd convinced him to help me shake the dust off the walls, as my mother always said, and we were already taking a break to cuddle on the couch. It felt natural for us to be this close to each other, spooned against each other's bodies, effortless and without negotiation. We'd been together since we were fresh out of college, more than ten years, married for the last two. Childless, we focused intensely on our careers, Richard's in biotech and mine in nursing. We were similar but different in every way, our professional lives an easy example. We'd always been happy, I believe as a result more of our differences than our similarities, but ever since the sleepy bliss of our honeymoon had dissipated, I'd felt a gnawing uncertainty about our future.

Richard had wanted to get married -- I didn't. Richard had fought hard to change my mind and had ultimately won because I wondered out loud, *How different could it be than our sinful cohabitation?* Maybe I preferred living in sin because I never became comfortable with being married to my boyfriend. The irony is that my parents are actually forty-six years married and proud of it; Richard's father was a philanderer and her mother, once divorced from him, was married three more times, including one where the guy beat her up. How could Richard, of all people, seek solace in the grips of legal matrimony? And how could I not?

When Richard got down on one knee and told me he loved me and wanted to marry me, it was right here in this living room at this cabin, two feet away from were we curled together. I stared at that spot now, glowing in the light of the fire, and remembered my utter panic as each nobly intended word staggered from his nervous mouth. He knew I was anti-marriage. But he said to me, "Sweetie, marriage is a concept you shy away from -- I know that. But this isn't a concept -- this is me, in the flesh, wanting you, in the flesh, to join with me to take on the world." I had studied his earnest face and his eyes nearly overflowing with hope and I'd sunk to my knees and said, "I want to take on the world with you."

Nine months later, we were married and the change I kept hoping to feel within myself, something that told me this decision was correct, never came to be. The day of our wedding was glorious and so was our subsequent trip to Italy's Amalfi Coast, but my ring finger felt burdened by the extra weight and a sadness grew in my heart with each passing day. I loved Richard -- there was no doubt about that -- but I hated our new definition -- *married couple*. As we lay on the couch together, I fiddled with my rings and frowned.

"What do you want to make for dinner?" Richard asked into my hair.

I sighed. "You decide."

"What if I decide to make hamburger helper?" he teased.

"I'd know you were probably going to have to grill those steaks instead because we didn't bring hamburger helper," I said, a bit snappish. "And we don't have hamburger helper because we do not have a four-year-old picky eater with us."

Richard shifted beside me, forcing me to sit up and look at him. "Sweetie..." he began, his face drawn.

"What?" I asked defensively.

"Talk to me," he said.

I ducked my eyes and chewed on the inside of my lip. "I don't think I'm happy," I said after a brief silence.

Richard's eyes flashed. "What?"

"I don't think I'm happy," I repeated, appreciating the honest ring the words had in my head.

Richard drew in a deep breath and exhaled. "How long have you felt like this?" he asked.

"A long time," I said.

"Are you unhappy being with me?" he asked a little too loudly.

"I love you," I said simply.

"But you're still unhappy."

I nodded. "I'm ungrateful. You give me everything. You are everything -- everything I ever wanted. But I can't help feeling the way I feel."

Richard leaned away from me and shook his head. "What do you want? A divorce? Should we move to Spain? Do you want to adopt a baby or get a dog? Go back to school? What will make you happy?"

His words fell over me like an unexpected avalanche. I shrugged and stared into the fire. "I don't know. I just know that something has to change."

"How can you not know what will make you happy, babe?" Richard asked, his voice at a simmer.

I looked him in the eye but pressed my lips firmly together. Around me, all I could see was unattended layers of dust and damp.

First paragraph by Jared Bieschke

Everyone's a Critic

"That's a terrible first line," said the eighteen-year-old Emerson student.

Elgin Summerfeld slumped in his chair and avoided eye contact with the girl dressed in a mini skirt that used to be part of a slutty maid costume and a men's t-shirt cut into a halter top, her hair short and dyed an electric blue. She, however, stared relentlessly at him with piercing green eyes and tossed the pages back across the table.

"Get a clue, Dad," she added, sliding back her chair and stomping her booted feet out the back door.

Elgin sat there, defeated, as his pages blew off the table in random orders, one falling unceremoniously into the dog's water bowl. "Well, that's that," he said.

"That's what, dear," his third wife Maya said, breezing into the kitchen.

"My writing career," he said. "It's over."

Maya eyed him suspiciously. "Did that ungrateful disaster tell you that?" she asked.

"Maya, please don't start..." Elgin begged.

Maya picked up a pair of tongs and started clacking them together as she turned on a burner on the stove. "*Ungrateful disaster*," she hissed, slamming a pan on the burner.

"She's creative, though, you have to admit that much," Elgin said meekly. "She wrote that brilliant piece about the time traveler who stalked himself through time, remember? You liked it..."

Maya sighed and added some olive oil to the pan. "I liked when she was going to live in the dorms at that overpriced *art* school."

Elgin shrugged. "It's just better to have her at home for the first year. She's so sensitive and I'm not sure dorm life would have worked realistically."

"You're worried about reality with that child?" Maya snorted, chopping up some mushrooms -- and then onions and then green peppers -- to add to the pan. "This is the same girl who got a tattoo of Superman in a tutu on her ass cheek? I can't say I'd worry so much about her being able to tough it in a dorm full of people like her."

"OK, so it saved me some money," Elgin said. "But I also thought she could help me with my writing..."

Maya clucked her tongue. "Just like her mother, that girl. I never saw you turn into a bigger coward than when Janice showed up at graduation. An adult woman with a hoop hanging out of her nose, who does she think she's kidding? I don't even want to think about the leather apparatus she surely owns."

Elgin shifted uncomfortably in his chair. "I'm not afraid of Janice," he said.

Maya laughed uproariously. "And my grandfather's Joseph Stalin," she said in an especially thick Spanish accent.

That was one of Maya's favorite sayings -- Elgin hated when she said it, mostly because he was fairly certain Joseph Stalin was a distant relative of his, a painful truth for him.

"Anyway, I didn't even talk to Janice at the graduation," he muttered.

"No, how could you? You were sweating profusely in an air conditioned room and stared at the exit signs the entire time. You barely spoke to *me* and I know you're not afraid of *me*," she said, leaning over to kiss his bald head.

Elgin folded his arms across his chest. "I wasn't sweating because of Janice," he said. "It was that new heart pressure medication..."

"You and your medication," Maya said, her voice rolling as much as her eyes. "What fifty-year-old man takes so many medications? You need to take better care of yourself, *mi amor*."

He watched her pull steaks out of the refrigerator and he sighed. "Yes, dear," he said, slumping his hand against his cheek.

"Well, you can say you're not afraid of your first wife, but I'm a woman and a *Latina* and that makes me especially qualified to call you out on your bullshit. Janice is your Boogeyman. Every night you have a twitchy sleep, I know that woman has slithered into your subconscious."

"There's no convincing you otherwise, so I won't try," Elgin said, his eye drifting to the page from his story now fully marinated in dog bowl water.

"That daughter of yours," Maya began, snapping her tongs once more, "is the spitting image of her mother. And she controls you just as easily."

His chin fell against his chest once more, but as his third wife went on explaining all of the ways he was emasculated by his eighteen-year-old daughter, his eyes drifted to one of the pages that had not blown off the table and he read quickly:

It had never mattered to him before that he was spending this time alone, so near the horizon he could nearly feel the embrace of the sun, but now that he realized that the zombie apocalypse was real and he was truly the last real man on this sad planet, it made him lay down and take the peaceful nap he'd never been able to take before, not with all those women talking at him all the time.

Suddenly, his eyes brightened and his head tilted back in a full-bellied laugh. Standing up, he pulled the page from the water bowl and shook it out.

"What are you doing?" Maya asked, interrupting her own stream of conscious babbling to check in with the scene before her.

"I"m going to go work on some revisions before I submit this to *The New Yorker*," he said with a twinkle in his eye.

"Even though your artsy daughter from the overpriced writing school said it stunk?" Maya asked, her eyebrows cocked.

Elgin shrugged. "She only read the first line. What does she know?" he asked, exiting the kitchen and returning to his home office where he could hide in the fantasy of his fiction for a little while at least.

First line by Tom Lada

Disruption

The sunshine was as brutal as his headache, but he stumbled, squinting, onward to answer the indefatigable doorbell. How long had it been ringing? Throwing the door open, his already surly mood grew even more sour.

"Mrs. Perkins," he said shortly.

His next door neighbor stood haughtily on his front porch in a housecoat thrown over her nightgown, tattered pink bedroom slippers on her gnarled old feet. "Jonathan, I don't want to have to ask you again," she said stiffly, the hint of a southern accent coating her words.

He set his jaw and pressed his hand flat against the doorjamb. "Ask me about what?"

"Roaring through the neighborhood at all hours of the night blasting music in your car," she said, as if it should have been overwhelmingly obvious.

To him, it was not so obvious. This batty old broad came knocking at his door at least twice a week lodging some kind of complaint about him. Three days ago, she'd stood in the same place and admonished him for allowing his black lab Mister to pee in a yard that did not belong to him. Last week, it was something about grilling outdoors after nine o'clock at night. This woman was limitless and even creative in her critiques of her neighbors. And it might be especially irksome if she was just targeting him, but this woman was infamous for knocking on everyone's door at some point during a given week. His was usually the only porch where she was still in her pjs and slippers, the added benefit of being her next-door-neighbor, he presumed.

"Mrs. Perkins, I do apologize," he said dryly.

"You do understand the meaning of *disruptive*, Jonathan, don't you?" she pressed.

He nodded slowly, the pounding in his head gaining steam.

Truth be told, he didn't even really remember blasting his car stereo the previous night. He did remember thinking he shouldn't be driving as he got behind the wheel, so maybe he turned up the music to keep himself from totally blacking out.

He'd had a rough night.

As a favor to a friend, he'd agreed to attend a book discussion about a new novel by a first time writer, a notion he considered charming since he'd once been in those shoes, and showed up at the bookstore with his notebook in hand and the general plot still fresh in his mind after giving the novel a quick read. As the time for the discussion crept nearer, he noticed that the only people in this gathering were book store employees plus two genuine patrons, one of whom was toting her granddaughter. After delaying the start of the discussion for a few minutes to accommodate never-appearing stragglers, the author, a nervous middle-aged woman with tight black spiral curls, assumed her place at the head of the group and began with a brief history of her own life, including her literary experience as an advice columnist for the Boston Globe in the 80's, before reading a few excerpts from the novel and then bashing her editor and her agent for making her change the cover art and the title from what *she* wanted to what *they* wanted. At some point along the way, she asked if there were any writers in the group, and he'd reluctantly raised his hand. She beamed at him and proceeded to give him advice for novel writing, should he ever want to try it out, including suggesting he write biographies of all his characters, make timelines, and, all-importantly, *write with an eraser handy*. He groaned inwardly the entire time, desperately wanting to say, "Ma'am, I have a master's degree in writing, have published three successful novels, and write a regular column in *Poets & Writers*," but he didn't. Instead, he nodded politely and pretended to take notes. The two other spectators at this event consisted of an Asian woman who didn't seem to speak English but who sat and videoed the entire presentation with her point and shoot camera and the possibly-senile older woman with the small child. The grandmother waited until the author asked if there were any questions and then launched into a story that a) was not a question and b) was almost totally irrelevant. Meanwhile, her granddaughter stared dully at him as he took notes, her face unchanging when he offered her a smile. Boy, was that kid creepy. And also, there was no discussion of the book, just a synopsis and a reading and a lesson in Creative Writing 101.

The first moment he could, he bolted to his car and threw it in drive. He showed up at Flannigan's Pub in six minutes and thirteen seconds and was resting comfortably on a barstool with a Maker's on the rocks four minutes after that. His ex-girlfriend Meryl was the bartender and she leaned over sympathetically and kissed his forehead after he'd vented for awhile.

"We can't all have successful book tours like you, Johnny," she said.

No one but Meryl called him *Johnny*.

"What're you writing now?" she asked.

It took him four more Maker's on the rocks to tell her the details of his latest project, a love story between a man and a ghost, and by the time he was trying to explain his *original* ending and the *organic* ending that was coming out instead, he blinked and swore there were two of her, his beautiful Meryl. How he had so monumentally fucked this one up? How could he have ever thought he'd find a better woman? How could he have found so many reasons to act jealous and shut her out? It was only when he was especially sober or especially drunk that he ever bothered to stare at the giant diamond on her finger and taste the bitterness in his mouth.

"The ghost dies at the end," he said sadly, his eyes absorbing the flashes from the rock.

"Johnny, maybe it's time for you to go," Meryl said softly.

He threw sixty dollars cash on the bar and slid of his seat. "Yeah," he said.

"Let me call you a cab," she said, her hand already on the phone.

"I'll walk," he lied as he pressed out the door.

Revving his engine, he sped through the upper-class suburbs he called home, screeching into his driveway, and parking crookedly in his garage, the only telltale sign that he'd driven drunk, and rested his head against the steering wheel for a moment or two, half-cursing his safe arrival. With his body in traction, he might feel justified in hurting so much. With his body in traction, he might be able to rehabilitate himself. Crawling into bed, alone again, the rush of the thrill-ride home dissipated and he was numb and unresponsive for hours, a self-diagnosed coma patient.

And now this. Mrs. Perkins. Disrupting his misery.

"Yes, I understand the word 'disruptive,'" he said, pronouncing each syllable precisely.

"I would think so with all those fancy books you keep writing," she said, her eyes flicking over him skeptically as if maybe he didn't actually write the books himself.

"I'll be more courteous in the future," he said as he closed the door in her face.

Sealed back inside, he closed his eyes and slumped to the floor with visions of brick walls hurdling towards his throbbing head.

First line by Jared Bieschke

Today

Most days I am perfectly content -- excited even -- to venture out into the world for my job and my social life, but today finds me enviously eyeing my beloved white cat perched in her sunny window, a grueling itinerary of sleeping and grooming ahead of her, as I try to navigate an exit from my apartment with no free hands. It's Ashley's birthday today so I've got a long tupperware full of pink frosted cupcakes and after work, I'm hitting the gym with Carl and Molly, so my backpack is full of clothes to get sweaty in as well as my sneakers, and as if that wasn't enough, I've got a tote bag slung over my left shoulder that has my lunch, a book, and some folders I need for the evaluations I am to perform on my employees today. But, yeah, I still can't even get out the door, so I'm not sure how any of this will happen. Shifting the cupcakes into one hand, I twist the knob and glance back at my cat, her eyes half-closed in the morning sun.

"Lucky bitch," I mutter as I make my way out into the hall and down the stairs.

Outside, I barely even register how beautiful it is as I realize I am oh-so-close to missing the bus. Oh yeah. I also have to take the bus today. Usually, my boyfriend drives me, but he didn't come home last night, instead sending me 2:30AM text that said, "Drunk, sleep, bye," so I'm on my own today it seems. I make it to the stop on time, somehow managing not to fall over or drop anything, and luckily I get a seat. Sometimes this bus is crazy packed in the morning -- today it's only mildly packed. I sit near the front. I like it up there so I can listen to the driver talk to people, both fellow passengers and on the radio to other drivers. I think it's character revealing. I always tell people I wish I'd studied to be a sociologist -- this kind of stuff is way too fascinating to me to be a hobby. But instead, I ran out of money and dropped out of college, so I manage a franchised retail store in a mall. We sell cards and crap. Thank you for shopping here. The bus drops me off right in front of the brick exterior of the mall and I pause for a moment to re-balance myself. Looking up at the building, I think for a moment about the subtle difference this concept of "mall" in the city is to ones I grew up near in the suburbs. All the same terrible stores with only a third of the parking.

This mall is three levels. My store is on the first one. We're located between an athletic shoe store and a cell phone outlet. Prime. I have to set most of my belongings down in order to unlock the grate and slide inside. From this point on, I just kick the tupperware of cupcakes out ahead of me. I feel strangely unburdened.

I enjoy these early mornings in my store, alone, before the mall opens, before my slew of employees shows up. I leave the cupcakes on the back counter where everyone is sure to see them and set a sign that says, "Happy Birthday, Ash!" on it. For good measure, I draw three balloons in the background. Sitting at my desk, I shove my backpack underneath and pull my tote bag into my lap. I withdraw the employee files I intended to fill out last night but didn't. I also withdraw my phone. I never texted my boyfriend back last night. There didn't seem to be a point. I consider responding now, but I don't do that either. I'll see him when I see him, I guess. Instead of thinking more about him, I move on to the rituals of opening my store. Within half an hour, other employees start to arrive, sleepy and yawning, including the birthday girl who squeals when she sees her treats.

"Share if you want," I tease her in a singsong voice.

She's nineteen today and exceptionally pretty. My boyfriend once hit on her in front of me without even realizing what he was doing -- as evidenced by the vibrant degree of red his face turned when those of us witnessing his "smooth moves" burst into laughter.

"Babe, you can't *how you doin'* a girl seven years younger than you who works for your girlfriend -- *especially* not when that girlfriend is standing there!" I'd howled.

But, yeah, she's a hottie, so who could blame him? Today she is so close to violating dress code in an extra-short skirt. I nearly comment on it. But I don't. Instead, I lean back in my desk chair. It's her birthday for chrissakes.

I'm still working on paperwork in the back when my assistant Shana comes in, late, as usual.

"How was last night?" she asks casually.

"Good," I say.

"Hungover?" she asks.

"Nope," I reply.

"Cool," she says before heading out onto the sales floor to see what the part timers are doing.

Shana and I have a love/hate relationship. We've worked together for nearly four years now and there are very few things we don't know about each other. I usually tell people she's like my sister -- because she's family, I will always be there for her, but do I actually enjoy her company? I'm never really sure. Today I appreciate her, though, in that she doesn't ask specifics about last night. She doesn't have to -- she can probably smell the truth on me.

As if the mere mention of last night could cause ears to burn, my phone vibrates in my bag and I see a text from my boyfriend. *Home now.* I don't respond to this one, either. He's probably already back to sleep, anyway. He's a bartender and a drummer in a pretty decent metal band, so he rarely experiences daylight anymore. I turn my phone completely off and drop it in the tote bag.

I spend the better part of the morning and early afternoon calling my employees back into the office one by one to talk to them about job performance. It's the same conversation over and over again -- *You do these three things really well. These are three areas you could improve in. You're getting a twenty-five cent per hour raise now. Thank you. Next!* -- and I silently curse the franchise owner, a rich old dude named Jeremiah who lives in a nearby condo overlooking the river, for making me do this every year. Why can't he just give everyone their piddly raise and move on?

I tell Shana I'll do her evaluation after I go to lunch as I breeze by her, cupcake in hand. My cell phone's back on and in my pocket as I make my way to grab a coffee and find a seat outside. There are several new messages and emails but I scan them in search of one in particular.

Love you.

There it is. I smile and ignore the rest. I spend my break people watching, wondering why the hurriers are hurrying, why the people slumped over tables are so down, what is making those women laugh so hysterically, what that probably-new mom is thinking as she pushes the baby buggy inside. I wonder if anyone is watching me. I wonder what they see.

Back inside, I call Shana back into my office to conduct her evaluation. She's my only full time employee, so her raise is generally higher and more performance-based, so I take this one a bit more seriously. Besides the fact that she's *always* late, she's a rockstar assistant. We spend maybe ten or fifteen minutes discussing her goals for the previous year and her goals for the year to come and when professionalism had seemed to reach its max, she transition-smiles at me.

"So?" she says.

I shrug and can't hide my smirk.

"You know you have to tell him, right?"

My gaze drifts off to the side of her. "Yeah," I say.

"OK," she says. "I'm gonna go to lunch then."

Shana is the only one who knows I am cheating on my boyfriend. Not even my closest friends know it -- but my work-sister does. I can't hide anything from her. She'd actually been relieved to discover the news -- she hates my boyfriend, always has.

"He's a drunk fuckwit mess," she'd say, glee edging her voice. "*Anyone* else would be trading up."

The new guy -- Will -- is definitely cut from a finer cloth. He works in the mayor's office and gets regular haircuts and thinks it is acceptable to have three beers and call it a night. I had met him a few weeks ago when I was waiting for my boyfriend to get off work on a rare occasion when he wasn't closing. Sitting alone at the bar, I was playing Words with Friends on my phone and ignoring everyone. My boyfriend was on a re-stock run down in the basement when Will approached me. We couldn't have spoken for more than five minutes, but there was something kinetic about the experience, so when he'd asked me for my number, I gave it to him without hesitation, and then watched him leave. Two minutes later, my boyfriend, buzzed from yet another round of tequila shots, slung an arm around me and asked if I was ready to go.

I was ready to go.

I took the keys from him that day and drove us home and by the time I tucked him into bed, I'd already gotten a text from Will. We got together the next day and were sleeping together by the fourth. Will doesn't know I live with my boyfriend. Since he is allergic to cats, it makes it all that much easier to keep him away from my apartment. And since my boyfriend spends so many nights out, often crashing elsewhere, it never is a problem to make a date with someone else. And for the icing on the cake, I deleted my Facebook page shortly after meeting Will so there could be no internet stalking snafus. When friends noticed my account was deactivated, I muttered something about privatizing my life and not living on the internet, and most people left me alone.

But Shana. I couldn't hide the truth from her. She noticed a difference in me instantly and, in her subtle way, pried the story out of me. She begged me to meet Will, so I made the introduction happen.

"This one is great," she said when he got up to buy us another round.

And now he is sending me *Love you* text messages.

Of course, I don't respond to his text, either.

After work, I meet my friends Carl and Molly at the gym to take a spin class and lift some weights. At some point we'd all worked together before -- they work together still -- so we spend most of our time bitching about people who we know in common. The only reason I could even stand it is they like to do their complaining in tandem with a solid workout. Today, though, all I can think about is what comes after the gym. My boyfriend has a show tonight and a bunch of our friends will be there -- but Will has also asked me if I'd like to come over while he cooks me a near-gourmet meal. I had vaguely agreed to both of these things, leaving enough wiggle room to get out of one or the other if I wanted.

Once the workout is complete, Molly cajoles me into a rare trip to the sauna. As we sit in the heat and don't speak to each other, I think back to my cat luxuriating in the sun and feel a bit like her for a moment or two. It's only now that I realize how exhausted I am.

Molly kindly gives me a ride home after we extract ourselves from that comfort zone. In my apartment alone, I take a long hot shower and when I return to the living room, I see my boyfriend's left some new lyrics out on the coffee table:

She's what's fierce and beautiful about this night

She's what gives me the strength to fight
I never say things to her right
I never tell her she grips my sight

He's scribbled them out, but I can still read them. Just then, my phone rings and I see it's Will calling. I don't pick up. Instead, I curl up on the couch beside my cat. I will follow her passive lead for at least today.

First line by Jennie Siegel

The Dragon

Everyone knows that dragons do not exist -- but the one in front of me seemed to disagree with that statement.

"Fix my tail," said the dragon.

"Sure," I said, doing the best I could.

The dragon grinned shyly at me and grabbed my hand. His fingers -- if that's what you call them -- wove awkwardly with mine, but I did my best to hold on. I didn't want to be rude. It was my first play date with a dragon, after all, and I wanted to fit in.

"Let's go on that slide," the dragon said.

"Sounds good," I replied, allowing myself to be dragged by the beast.

"You watch me, OK?" the dragon said, swinging his tail as he walked away from me over to the ladder that would bring him to the slide platform.

"I'm right here," I said.

The dragon nodded at me and, after making the climb, turned and pumped his clawed fists in the air. "ROAR!" he bellowed.

Everyone turned and stared at him in awe. They had never seen a dragon either, I'm guessing. I raised my arms in the air in a measure of solidarity. The dragon saw me and pointed and grinned. Then he whooshed down the slide and lightly scampered back over to me to give me a high five.

"I'm gonna try the purple slide now," the dragon said, rushing back over to the intricate jungle gym.

I watched the dragon maneuver among the regular children, occasionally inciting little yips of panic when he'd flash his rows of teeth, but the children always came around to find a way to grin and swat at the green monster before them.

"See? I'm not so scary," the dragon said more than once.

I smiled and thought of the first moment I'd seen him when I had panicked a little. That memory seemed so small and foreign and soon to be forgotten. I was learning to love this dragon, this mysterious beast, this misnomered monster.

He said to me, "Once people understand I don't want to hurt them, they usually like me. I'm a nice dragon. I just want to play like the kids do."

I nodded and took him seriously. "I think they get that."

"Yeah," the dragon said. "Yeah, I think so, too. But it's sometimes hard for people to want to play with me."

We were eating apples and sitting on side-by-side swings.

"Really? I'd think most kids would like a friendly dragon," I said.

The dragon shrugged. "I guess *most* do. But not *all*. Some kids pull at my tail and say it's fake."

"What do you say when that happens?" I asked.

"I say that it's my tail and they're not to pull on it," the dragon said simply. "They usually stop. But sometimes they call me names when they walk away."

"Like what kind of names?" I asked.

The dragon shrugged again. "I dunno. Different things. They think I'm lying about being a dragon. And some of them call me a dinosaur, which is just wrong. Everyone knows dinosaurs are extinct."

I studied the dragon's serious face and concurred. "Yeah, *everyone* knows that."

The dragon hopped off the swing. "Let's go back to my house now," he said.

"OK," I said, taking his outstretched hand.

Within the hour, the dragon was tucked in bed with his eyes slammed shut and a slight shuttering sigh of a snore fluttering through his lips. He was a peaceful monster, a mythical creature of kindness. I closed the door to his room and tip toed down to the living room to wait for the dragon to wake.

"After my nap, I'll show you how I breathe fire," the dragon had promised as he'd shifted into sleep.

I couldn't wait to see that.

First line by Sean OhEigeartaigh

Opposites

Did you know chows are the most likely dog to turn against their owners? I saw a special about it on Animal Planet over at my aunt's house a few weeks ago and it hasn't left my mind. My next door neighbors have a chow mix named Armadillo who growls every time he sees me and my mom says it's because he's being protective of Mr. and Mrs. Sampson. I look at my mom and say, "I'm eleven and I take ballet. How threatening do I seem?" But my mom says it's in Armadillo's nature. I don't think she *knows* the full extent of Armadillo's nature, not like Animal Planet and I do at least.

I don't have a dog, but I want one. My mom says we'll get one if we move out of the apartment building, which we might do in the spring or summer. It's winter now. I walk home from the bus stop after school and my faded pink snow boots squish in slushy snow. They're faded pink because they're from last year and my toes cramp up inside of them a little, but my mom asked if I wanted new ballet slippers or new boots and I'd picked ballet. I only had to wear the boots when I was outside, after all, which was not that often since I detest being in the cold. I tell my mom all the time that what I really want is to get a dog and live someplace sunny. She always smiles and says she wants that, too, so maybe in the spring or the summer, all of our dreams will come true. She asks me, "Sadie, what kind of dog do you want?" And I say, "The opposite of Armadillo."

In the same Animal Planet show, they said that dalmatians have long memories, like elephants, and if someone was mean to one, say, as a puppy, and then they were separated for years and years, if that person came around, the dalmatian would remember that unkindness and stay away from the one who'd hurt him. I think this is fascinating and I wish the Sampsons had a dalmatian instead of a chow mix because I want to see if this is true. Not that I want to be mean -- I would be so nice to a cute, spotted dalmatian and I'd want to see if he would remember my kindness. If he can remember cruelty, he should remember the opposite, right? Animal Planet didn't say, but I think it seems logical.

I started taking ballet when I was four and I used to hate it. I wanted to learn to play the piano but my mom said that I would make more friends if I did ballet, so she ignored my tantrums and kept taking me to practice. She said she took ballet when she was little, too, and as long as I didn't keep taking ballet when I was a teenager, it would be a healthy life choice. I didn't really understand what she meant by that, but I liked the smile she'd get on her face when she'd say it, so I didn't ask her to explain it to me. And I did learn to love ballet. My best friends are Mary Jo and Trina -- who we call *Trina the Ballerina*, of course -- and we've danced together our whole careers. We like to call it a *career* because it sounds grownup and it makes the adults laugh in an easy way. Mary Jo has a cat named Mr. Whiskers who's all black except for one white foot and Trina has a french bulldog named Pierre.

Today when I get home from school, Mrs. Sampson stops me in the hallway and says, "Sadie, come in here, please."

Mrs. Sampson is enormously tall and has short very curly hair and every time I look at her, my head drops all the way back to see her fully as my mouth hangs open. "Why?" I ask.

"Your mom asked me to watch you for a bit this afternoon," she says, ushering me in the door.

I hear Armadillo barking in the other room and it makes me jump.

"Don't worry about him," Mrs. Sampson says, waving her hand towards her shut bedroom door. "He'll settle down in a minute."

"Why's he in there?" I ask, cautiously eyeing the door.

"I know you're a little afraid of him," Mrs. Sampson says simply. "Can I get you a snack? Or some juice?"

"I'm not afraid of him," I say weakly.

Mrs. Sampson chuckles. "He's all bark and no bite, really," she says.

I open my mouth to tell her how wrong both Animal Planet and I know she is, but I close it just as quickly. "Where's my mom?" I ask.

Mrs. Sampson is pouring me a glass of orange juice. "She went somewhere with your father, sweetie," she says, ushering me to her kitchen table as she cuts up an apple.

"You like peanut butter, right?"

My mouth hangs open and I know she's told me something she wasn't supposed to tell me. "She's with my dad?" I repeat.

"MmmHmm," Mrs. Sampson murmurs.

The last time I'd seen my dad was when we moved out of our old apartment and into the one next to the Sampsons. I was barely four then -- I hadn't even started ballet yet. I had cried so hard when we left him behind, but my mom said we had to go. Her face had bruises and one arm was in a sling as she hoisted me up and out the door and after awhile, I stopped asking when I could see him again and was surprised to learn my mom liked to sing and smile and skip around the park with me. Before, she'd never been like that -- always sad and crying and maybe even afraid. But in our new apartment, she was happy and she took me to dance class and she said one day we could get a puppy.

Why is my mom somewhere now with my dad?

"When's she coming back?" I ask Mrs. Sampson who shrugs and replies, "She said she'd be back soon."

Mrs. Sampson lets me watch whatever I want on TV so I find an episode of *Pretty Little Liars* and watch that and then ask for a space to sit and do my math and English homework and by then Mr. Sampson is home from work and I hear them whispering in the kitchen and I see Mrs. Sampson make another phone call, probably to my mom, although it's so quiet, I can't hear her speaking. And I'm still there when it's dinner time and I'm still there when it's completely dark out and it's time for bed. Mr. and Mrs. Sampson glance at me nervously as I sit on their couch with my feet curled under me. I fall asleep there eventually and wake up with a blanket over me and a wet dog nose in my face. Armadillo is sniffing me all over and not growling, for once. Mr. Sampson whistles and the dog runs over to him.

"Sorry, Sadie, I'm just taking him out for a walk," he says.

"OK," I say, drawing the blanket up to my chin as they walk out the door.

I look at the clock. It's 11:30PM. I start to panic. Getting up, I go and find Mrs. Sampson in her room. She's sitting on the edge of her bed and she's got her cell phone pressed against her ear.

"Not since two this afternoon," she's saying before she looks up and notices me. "Let me call you back," she adds and then hangs up.

"Where's my mom?" I ask.

"I don't know, Sadie," Mrs. Sampson says.

I start to cry. "I want my mom!" I say.

"I know, sweetie," she says, hugging me to her. "She hasn't answered her phone all day and I don't really know any of her friends. Do you know who I could call?"

"My aunt Jessie lives in Fullbrook," I say. Fullbrook is the next town over. "I know her phone number by heart."

"Let's call her," Mrs. Sampson says, a hint of relief in her voice. "What's the number?"

I tell her and she gets Aunt Jessie's voice mail so she leaves a message and within five minutes, she calls back. I can hear her panic through Mrs. Sampson's phone, even without the phone pressed to my ear.

"She's coming to get you, Sadie," Mrs. Sampson says after she's explained what she knows.

"Thank you," I say in a very small voice.

It's just after midnight when Aunt Jessie arrives in the Sampson's apartment and she's out of breath and her face is really red from the cold.

"Get your things, Sadie," she says and then she looks at the Sampsons both, since Mr. Sampson and Armadillo had since returned from their walk. "I called the police. There's a restraining order against Darrell. They're looking for him right now. Thank you for watching Sadie and if you hear anything..."

"Don't worry about us. And please let us know..." Mrs. Sampson says, her voice trailing off.

I wish I had my teddy bear Goliath right now but he is locked in the apartment. As Aunt Jessie escorts me out the door, I ask her if she has a key and she says she does so we go in and pack some of my things in a bag and I grab hold of Goliath and she takes me to her car and drives me to her house. My aunt Jessie is five years younger than my mom and she is married to a rich man named Liam who bought her a sun conure named Rosie and an African Grey named Lucifer, which is another name for the devil, and I asked my aunt once why she liked birds so much and she said, "Because they're both pretty and smart, just like my Sadie." I had said, "*Collies* are pretty and smart," but Aunt Jessie just laughed and didn't say anything else.

In the car on the way, I want to ask so many questions, but something in the air tells me to keep quiet. My aunt looks fierce in the driver's seat, her jaw clenched and her hands gripping the steering wheel. Uncle Liam is standing in the front yard when we get to their house, a surprising sight at such a late hour. He's got his phone pressed against his ear and the free hand pressed into his hip. He has a lovely Irish accent and I have never seen him frown before this moment. Aunt Jessie has rolled her window down as we pull into the driveway.

"Anything?" she asks.

Uncle Liam shakes his head.

Aunt Jessie takes me inside and up to the guest bedroom. She sits me down on the bed and says, "Sadie, we don't know where your mom is but I don't want you to worry. Policemen are looking for her and she'll be OK. So you go to bed."

"What about school tomorrow?" I ask.

"No school tomorrow," she says hastily.

I start crying again. "OK," I say in a quiet voice. I have never felt so afraid before.

Aunt Jessie hugs me tightly. "Try and fall asleep, Sadie. I'm going to go talk to Uncle Liam for a minute and then I'll come read you a story or something if you need me to, OK?"

No one has read me a bedtime story in years, but I nod and then I climb into bed, still wearing my school clothes and clutching onto Goliath.

The next morning, I wake up and go down to the kitchen to find Aunt Jessie and Uncle Liam sitting at the kitchen table clutching cups of coffee. They both look so tired. I sit down beside Aunt Jessie who kisses me on top of the head.

"Morning, sweetie," she says.

"Did you find my mom yet?" I ask, even though I know the answer.

The answer to my question remains the same for the next three days. And for three days more after that. On the seventh day, Aunt Jessie brings me to the apartment to get some more of my things and we see Mr. Sampson leaving the building to take Armadillo for a walk. My eyes stick on them as they head down the block and I say to my aunt, "Remember that Animal Planet thing about chows?"

"What, Sadie?" Aunt Jessie asks, distracted by a text message on her phone.

"How on Animal Planet they said that chows are the most likely to turn on their people," I say.

"Uh huh," she replies, busily typing a response to her text.

"Is my dad a chow?" I ask slowly.

Aunt Jessie stops and stares at me, a sudden tear in her eye. "Yes," she says, the word snapping shut.

I trail behind her on our way up to my apartment and I wonder when I'll be back to feeling the opposite of this.

First line by Justine Eachus

Adventureman

Every time I look up at the moonlit New Hampshire sky, I feel the adventurousness of the human spirit, and see the unlimited potential our lives have and that I crave and would reach out and grab -- if only I hadn't knocked up Becki Dupuis. She's in the house while I'm out here looking at the sky. Our daughter Morgan is one week old today and and I haven't slept more than two hours a night since her arrival. Really, I haven't slept well for months -- maybe nine of them -- but the level of depravity veers directly towards rock bottom these days. I used to be wild and bohemian, drinking all night, smoking all day, carefree and, god, happy! And now? Now I'm a husband and a father and it's knocked the wind out of my sails.

I met Becki maybe a year ago at a bar in Cambridge, Massachusetts. We'd both showed up to see the same band. She'd caught my eye because she wore a long gypsy skirt and a flowing white top with a yellow scarf tied in her curly black hair and she never stopped moving. It was like watching an underwater creature swim. It seemed like she knew many of the people in the room and it stirred a pot of jealousy in my stomach -- how come *I* didn't know her. Finally, I walked over to her and said, "Ever heard of Jeff Crosby?" She'd paused and smiled with slightly dilated eyes and then said, "The bassist?" I nodded at her. She pressed a finger against her nose and squinted at me. "The original bassist for *this* band?" she said. I nodded again. "Fuck yeah, I've heard of him," she said. "Well, he's pleased to meet ya," I said, sticking my hand out. She jumped up and down and then went straight for the bear hug, leaving my hand to flap in the breeze. "Holy shit!" she yelled. Then she added, "Jeff, I'm Becki and I am at your service."

It had been such a long time since I'd played the musician card on a girl, but it just felt right in that moment, you know? I had to meet this girl and I knew that *this* was my ticket to the pony show. So I hung around with her for the second half of the last set and it wasn't until near the end that I felt a forceful tap on my shoulder and I turned around to see the very angry face of my girlfriend Patty staring meanly at me.

"What the fuck, Jeff?" she said, her arms folded across her chest.

By then, I was wasted and a little stoned, thanks to my new friend, and I had kind of forgotten that Patty was there. Patty, by the way, was my girlfriend of three years. We lived together, sort of, and were maybe getting engaged soon. At least, that was the plan before she stormed over to me at the bar where I was getting wasted with another girl -- who was both younger and hotter -- and I may or may not have had my hands indecently placed on her when Patty decided to confront. It's a little blurry. What *isn't* blurry is Patty bitch slapping me across the face and then storming out of the bar.

This is the straw. This is the camel's back. This is how it broke.

Everyone stopped what they were doing and watched as I slid to the ground in a ball of insobriety and start to giggle like an insane person. But Becki, she knelt down beside me and said, "Jeff, it's OK, man," and she helped me back to my feet in time for the band to play their last song and then two encores and then I went home with Becki Dupuis.

It's kind of a terrible *how we met* story, but it's our story.

And what's worse is Patty and I didn't even officially break up for another two months after that -- Becki and I just kept hooking up and then I'd go home to Patty's apartment and hook up again. Becki, she knew the deal, but Patty didn't and I hope she never does. She's a really nice girl who was always a little too straight-and-narrow for me but who people like my parents and non-musician friends thought I should date. Anyway, I finally ended things by telling her that I needed to spend more time at home in New Hampshire working on my new music projects and actually showing up to my job and stuff and that I would always love her but I didn't really see myself wanting to get married or have kids and I knew that she did, so I was doing the right thing and letting her go. And we'd hugged and cried together -- me, too, with genuine tears -- and then I'd left her apartment with all of my things, gotten in the car, and gone over to Becki's where I'd dumped all of the stuff I'd taken from Patty's. And then after we smoked some pot for awhile, we went online and booked a trip neither of us could afford to go backpacking in Costa Rica for two weeks.

This was the sort of thing that would *never* happen with Patty and me but happened immediately and with regular consitency with Becki and me -- we partied together and then we'd get these crazy ideas about where an adventure could take us or should take us or would take us and then we were off and running before we'd even pieced together complete scenarios. This was my *dream* girl. She was carefree but still loving and loyal and OK with adding an extra person in the bed when the spirit moved us and I had never been happier in my entire life.

And then it happened. The day came, five and a half months into our relationship, when Becki suggested we road trip, just the two of us, to Mt. Techumseh to hike to the summit and maybe camp out. It was an easy trip by our already daring standards, but it was a nice summer day and I had already blown off work, so what the hell! And so hike we did and when we reached the top, we took a moment to breath in the beautiful view before Becki took my hands, sucked in a deep breath, looked into my face, and said, "Jeff, we're pregnant."

What did I do? I did what every asshole on the planet would do in this moment. I said, "Are you sure it's mine?"

But Becki, man, she's cool as shit, so she didn't shove me off the mountain like most women would have. She simply nodded slowly and said, "Yes. We can get a test to be sure, though."

I looked into her face and saw such hope and light and love in that moment that for the briefest of seconds, I sincerely was thrilled. *Me, a father!* And then a moment later, the euphoria passed and I felt the weight of the goddamn world fall upon me. *Me, a father.*

"Let's hike back down and go and stay at my house tonight instead of camping," I said, grabbing our gear off the ground.

Becki chewed the inside of her lip and said, "OK."

From that moment on, our life together was different. We moved most of her stuff out of her Cambridge apartment -- that she shared with two guys and another girl and at least three cats -- and into my house in South Hampton, a place that stood empty if I wasn't there. I started going to my under-the-table job at the auto body shop on a much more regular basis and even asked my uncle to put me on the legit payroll so I could qualify for heath insurance. Becki got a job working in a veterinary office as a receptionist and nearly immediately adopted a Boston Terrier she named Sport. We were setting up a home and it brought a bright glow to Becki's cheeks and I tried to mirror her excitement, but part of me kept praying that when we got the paternity test done that it would turn out not to be my child.

It was my child.

So now what. She didn't have any health insurance and my uncle had finally managed to get me onto his, so I asked if he could help out my knocked up girlfriend but the only way to make it legit was to make *us* legit -- we had to get married. Our families basically staged an intervention (disguised as Thanksgiving dinner) where her parents and my parents and my uncle and her two brothers and my sister and our living grandparents all sat the two of us down and said, "Look. It's not just about the two of you any more." And when Becki and I had a minute to ourselves, we'd talked it through and decided it was for the best. So on December 1st, we got married with only those before-mentioned relatives present.

Our friends in the city half-knew what was going on. I had disabled my Facebook account as soon as I found out Becki was pregnant and she had changed her status to "In a Relationship" but left off the tidbit about being pregnant, and even being married, so only the people we chose to tell really knew. I kept thinking about Patty and how stunned she'd be that I'd broken up with her because I didn't want to get married and have kids and now look at me. And I kept thinking about Becki and how little I actually knew about her and I wondered if I loved her at all and if any of this was going to work out OK. I'd wake up in the middle of the night and see her sprawled out beside me, looking peaceful and even happy with a hand wearing a simple gold band on the ring finger resting on her slowly bulging belly and I would think, *God, what have I done?* Becki never seemed to have a fear or a doubt about any of it, embracing this change in her young life. Here she was, twenty-six and pregnant and married to a washed up musician she'd known for fifteen minutes and none of it seemed to phase her. This both confused and terrified me. Why wasn't she more worried? I was thirty-four and universally a mess -- I was a *guy*, not a *man*. I did nothing but worry all the time.

And now my daughter is born and she's small and pink and wrinkly and still not a human to me. I held her in the hospital like she was sculpture made of hot liquid glass shifting in my arms and I had asked that we name her *Morgan* after my favorite aunt who'd died a long time ago and not after *Bella* from *Twilight* like Becki had teased that she wanted to for the last month of the pregnancy.

"Morgan it is," Becki had said, scooping the child out of my arms and into her own.

And a week later, I'm just as uncomfortable as I ever was. Sitting outside, staring up at the spring sky, I am obsessed with its limitless space and how I can no longer be a part of it. I am here, forever, in this place, doing the right thing by the female beings who have turned my house into a home. I want to be grateful. I want to be happy. I want to wake up one day and feel alive in this new world of mine.

I want, I want, I want.

First line by Nate DiNardo

The Wife of the Alcoholic

"Feelings are there to be drowned in alcohol, not talked about!"

She didn't need to glance sideways at him to see that his finger was pointing in the air with his shoulder hunching towards his ear. She also didn't need to glance over to see he was already flicking his eyes towards her so she could chastise him like he knew she wanted to. She kept her eyes forward and her hands in the pockets of her coat as they continued their slow walk home. Once or twice she opened her mouth to give him what he wanted -- the sarcastic retort to his sarcastic retort, thus perpetuating the cycle, *their* cycle -- but she pressed her lips firmly together and stubbornly locked her response away. When had they become so predictable to each other? When did they become their own clichés? She sighed as he staggered into her and then ricocheted back off onto his own path and was both happy and sad at the same time to be the sober one in the party.

They walked a few blocks in near silence before he tried again. "I said, I won't talk about it."

"I heard you," she said, still with her gaze fixed forward.

"Well, aren't you going to tell me I have to talk about it?" he said.

"No," she said coolly.

He laughed. "What have you done with my wife?" he asked. "She'd make me talk."

"I haven't done anything with your wife," she said. "I just don't want to make you talk about it. I want you to talk about what you want and that's the end of that."

"Really?" he said in a dubious tone. "And I'm supposed to believe you?"

"You can do what you want," she said. "Right now, I just want to walk the three remaining blocks to our building and then go straight to bed."

"Really," he repeated.

"Really," she said firmly.

"Well," he said. "Well."

She tried to pick up the pace but it was difficult when he was so unstable. She bit back a snide remark about how he needed to learn to say *"No thank you"* when the whiskey came out, that it was OK to decline, that whiskey made him an unbearable disaster and could he, just once, think about her having to scrape him up off the floor when the liquor overloaded his brain and make apologies to the hosts whose wives would look sympathetically at her and say, "Your husband is a brilliant man," with the utmost of irony and seriousness all at once. After nearly thirty years together, she was used to the pitying looks, the tight lipped smiles, the rigid body language and it made her want to scream -- to scream at them, *"Stop offering him the booze, then!"* But she didn't. She just thanked them for a lovely evening and shrugged her husband into his coat.

Tonight's dinner party had been at a fellow professor's home where the theme had been wine and cheese pairing along with small plates that complimented the changing season -- hearty, warm, and heavy. After dinner, they'd settled into the den where a lively discussion about the upcoming election sparked a tone of controversy over, of all issues, same sex marriage.

"This is Massachusetts," her husband had pointed out. "It's legal here already anyway -- how can this be a persuading factor for you?"

"Because I think gay marriage is an abomination," a red-faced fellow academic had chortled.

"How is love an abomination?" her husband seethed. "How can the love of two people be disregarded simply because they have matching genitals?"

"Next you'll say brothers and sisters should be allowed to marry," the professor countered. "Fathers and daughters and first cousins, gettin' hitched."

"Be reasonable," her husband said.

"How is love an abomination?" the professor mocked.

Her husband opened his mouth only to close it again as someone else in the room piped up, "There are genetic implications to interbreeding that don't occur with homosexual couples..." and as the debate raged on, her husband sank deeper and deeper into his chair, his after dinner old fashioned clutched fiercely in his hands. She watched him with regard, waiting for the tell tale sign that they should leave before he shot molten lava of hate all over them.

He had a son who was gay. Twenty-seven-years-old, brilliant, handsome, and born out of wedlock, the result of an affair he'd had with colleague when they'd lived in Connecticut. None of his current colleagues knew about the boy and all of the struggles that their family had gone through because of him. On bad days, she referred to the boy as *the dirty secret*, a bitter pill that she'd managed to swallow only because he was out of sight/out of mind much of the time, but she knew her husband's mind festered with guilt on so many levels -- although mostly guilt over getting caught. A living breathing being is the most surefire way to uncover an affair and while she'd worked through it and deemed their marriage salvageable, there were always residual sticky-factors that turned into passive-aggressive punches in moments of emotional panic. She had only ever met the boy on a few occasions -- his high school graduation, his college graduation, and on his wedding day just a month ago -- and each time, it had been awkward and soul-piercing. The boy looked so much like her husband and it had pained her every time to see what this throw-away woman had born her husband when she hadn't produced any offspring at all. Listening to the party debate about gay marriage and watching her husband turn slack with intoxication made her inwardly furious on so many levels. How was *this* her life?

As they trudged up the final block to their building, he reached over and solidly took her hand, a gesture that made her stop and turn to face him. His face looked weathered and unhappy.

"I'm sorry," he said.

She felt her heart swell with unmanageable feeling. "Yes," she said, letting them linger in a locked stare for a few more moments before ending their journey home.

First line by Vinny Siegel

The Ugly Lights

Sometimes the best kind of birth control is good lighting. I see it all the time -- drunken people pairing off as the hour clicks closer to 2AM and, true, some of them escape before I have the chance to slam those overhead lights back on and ruin the illusion, but for those who remain, I feel like I'm doing my part to save the future of the human race. BAM! Bright lights. Outta nowhere. Look at her, buddy, really look at her. Do you want to be paying this twisted sister child support for the rest of your miserable life? I didn't think so. Thank you for the generous tip.

I've been a bartender at Clowd's here on Martha's Vineyard for, oh, ten or eleven years now. I'm pretty much the only one who's here year-round. I probably don't have to tell you how different it is between the long slow off-season and the short but boomin' summer months. Off-season, I know every person who walks in the door -- and can usually tell who they are by listening to their gait before they even make it all the way in -- but during the summer, it's a clusterfuck of god-knows-who. Clowd's is on a back road in Edgartown so you'd think we'd be hard to find but we're not and for one big reason: we're a favorite hangout of Samuel L. Jackson.

OK, so let me get real honest with you for a second. I have bartended at Clowd's for over a decade, easy, and I have never, not one time, seen let alone met Samuel L. Jackson. I don't even know if he's ever been to the island. But the guy who owns the joint has a cousin who's good friends with Samuel L's agent who got the big man to agree to say he hangs out at Clowd's. I guess he tweets about it sometimes or it's on his website or he wrote a glowing Yelp review or I dunno how he got the word out there, but it's one of the Vineyard's worst kept secrets that Samuel L. loves the chowder at Clowd's and so people come in, hoping to see him kicked back at the bar.

"Does he have his own room here?" asks at least half a dozen people every night.

"No, he usually sits over there," I say, pointing vaguely off in the distance.

I get paid extra for keeping the rumor alive. The whole thing's madness. Especially when we do have real celebrities coming in here all the time -- Larry David, Michael J. Fox, Chelsea Clinton, Adam Sandler, and Ted Danson, to name a few. Actually, both Larry and Ted hang out at Clowd's on a really regular basis but who is our celebrity draw? A guy who's never even set foot inside. Public relations is such a fuckin' scam.

Of course, so is dimming the lights in the bar and then serving alcohol. Some nights there is no better job in the world than mine. Watching the human drama unfold before me is pretty much the greatest reality television show I could ever hope to see. Little deals become big deals and big issues are sloshed aside or resolved with the clink of a glass. I love it. I'm hooked. Until the hour or so before closing time, I revel in the social dynamics around me. But when it gets close to do or die time, that's when I turn into big brother. I mean, I'm no buzz kill -- go out there, get laid, have fun -- but when it's desperation o'clock, I get involved. I have a bowl of condoms behind the bar that I will slide over along with closed tabs, which has the double effect of *thanks, man* and *oh shit, what was I thinking??* I also like to whip out a photograph of a wrinkly red faced baby wrapped in a blanket in its mother's arms to show some drunk horny youngsters before they slither out of the bar together. I like to say, "Have I shown you a photo of my baby? She cries all the time. Like, *all* the time." Yeah, I don't have a baby and it's a mean trick to play on kids who just wanna fuck, but, hell, as the only sober guy in the room, I think my judgement should count for something.

But the trick that works the best, industry wide, is flippin' on the ugly lights. Suddenly, princes and princesses are returned to their toad-like real-selves and the spell is broken. This is especially true with women and their friends. I can't tell you how many times a gaggle of ladies will be sitting together sipping their vodka cranberries and watching their solo sister out there getting macked on by some hot-toddy only to have those ugly lights come on to reveal the dude to be snaggle toothed or a bad dresser or a red head and one of those girls will always beeline over and snatch their girl up by the wrist and drag her right out. It happens literally every day and it's my favorite thing.

"Oh no you *don't*," says protective sister. "We are *out*."

Poor ugly bastard is left standing there with a condom in one hand the picture of my fake baby daughter in the other. It's just awesome.

One night, though, right near the end of the summer season, I flipped on the ugly lights and watched the usual scattering, and after chuckling about it for awhile, I leaned on the bar near Larry David, who had been drinking Scotch undisturbed for about two hours, and said to him, "Larry, for a guy in television, you gotta admit, there's no better show then when the ugly lights come on."

And you know what he said to me? He said, "I dunno. I thought the first few seasons of *Seinfeld* were pretty good TV."

First line by Chris Gray

Gwen Says

Loneliness surrounds my heart even though I am among the most intriguing people I have ever encountered. I just want someone to share it with, that's all. Life's selfish like that. I'm selfish like that. Occasionally, Gwen would look at me and say, "Bobby, if I didn't already love you, I wouldn't start now." I listened to everything she said in earnest. She was like my very own crystal ball -- she'd tell me what was going to happen and she was never wrong. I was in a bad place, that's what she meant. I was drifting alone.

I'd never been here before -- Atlantic City. Last night around midnight, I'd slammed the door on yet another fight with my lady-of-the-hour and gotten in my car. Didn't have a plan. Walking around the boardwalk, I still didn't really have a plan. I didn't like casinos and I hated the beach. But there's something about being in this kind of air -- the kind where getting high on hope is a thing -- and I guess I knew this is what I should be breathing right now. Plus, I like to people watch. People fascinate me. Even on my darkest days, I will stop and stare at the parade of people around me. Gwen says I do that because I want to identify with them somehow. She says I look for the humanity. But then she also says, "You always push past that, though, to see where the defects in that humanity lie. You like to find the buttons that could be pushed to make that person self-destruct." She says this kind of thing in a cagey way, indirectly pointing out that I do that sort of thing to myself and anyone I allow close to me. She used to be more direct about it. She used to say, "Bobby, you're fucking everything up." And I would listen. But after some time, I guess I stopped. I guess I didn't care anymore. Yeah, over time she became more and more passive aggressive, but that's because of me, not because of her.

About a year ago, I got my heart broken by a woman who was, quite frankly, too good for me. We didn't see things the same, not from day one, but that's kind of what made it all work. And then the closer we got, the more impressed I became with her. She was into yoga and used to lecture to me about my blocked chakra system, something that would be apparent to any old stranger walking by since I was the definition of a "mess" and she taught me some breathing exercises. They interfered with my smoke breaks, but otherwise were weirdly renewing. She made me see that there was more to life than streams of sarcasm and bottles of Jack. Maybe she wanted to help me -- save me. Maybe she realized it would never work -- I'm beyond saving. So she left me almost as quickly as she found me. We never even had sex, but I loved her -- loved her more than I loved anyone else I'd ever known in this lifetime. And once she was gone, I only got darker.

On the boardwalk in Atlantic City, I think about Gwen telling me I'm a co-dependent nightmare. "You've got to learn that who you are is OK. And if who you are isn't OK, then you need to fix that first before you can attach another life to your own." I never stopped being in love, but I also didn't stop the parade of useless relationships and Gwen was absolutely right. As I walk along all alone right now, I'm itching to find someone to sling my arm around, to tuck in beside me wherever I sleep tonight. If there isn't a warm life within reach, I am not alive. I tried to explain that to Gwen, but she wouldn't listen. "You can't identify through the lens of someone else. You have to be your own man, for chrissakes. How else will you even know if this is what you want? You don't even know *you*." I avoided her eye contact during these barrages. Mostly because she is right. Mostly because I don't have any intention of changing.

No matter what room I'm in, I'm alone, that's what Gwen would ultimately argue. Her words live in my head, after all, so I should know. Looking around at the people on the boardwalk, I turn my head to the left and I spit. No one even notices.

First few lines by Erin Good

One Love

I swear I'm never going to drink again. Sitting slumped in a plastic adirondacks chair on the porch off my third floor Cambridge apartment, I press my hand against my face and feel the heat from all of my mistakes in the past seven hours radiate against my palm. Staring dully at the soft haze of the July morning, I frown and want so much to blame the whiskey, but I thought of my Grandpa Jack's old saying, "When you're drinkin', then you're thinkin'," always said with an annoyingly exaggerate wink and followed by a customary slap on the knee. "The drunker you are, the realer you be," he would add if you would listen. I always listened.

This morning, I prop my feet up on the balcony railing and am thankful that at least my holier-than-thou cousin isn't around this weekend to see my utter demise at the hands of a drinking game I outgrew years ago. What thirty-year-old still plays drinking games? Maybe lots of thirty-year-olds, what am I saying? But not me. I drink to be social not to relive my college days. Last night, though, I was more-than-easily convinced to play a game of Eights. Come to think of it, it might have even been my idea.

For that, I blame Jon.

Before leaving for last night's party at my friend Celia's house, I had to make the big change -- I had to remove the "in a relationship with Jon Marcus" tag from my Facebook profile, something that seemed impossible until the events of the previous week. Jon and I had been together for nearly four blissful years, living together for the last three and a half, and so perfectly folded into each other's lives, I forgot there was life before meeting him. I was richly in love with him, almost at first sight, something I never believed was possible until I saw him walking towards me in a bar. He thought I was someone else he knew, but when I turned out to be not who he expected, that twist was enough to spark a conversation that lasted for years to come. He felt like part of my soul, part of my existence, part of my purpose in life. We talked about marriage and children and a summer house on Martha's Vineyard. But I was blinded by my side of it, it seems, because when it came crashing down on me, I was completely unprepared, like someone with a faulty seat belt in a car accident.

I didn't see he was growing distant and unhappy with our relationship. I thought it was aging -- he'd just hit the big three-oh a few weeks ago -- I thought it was unhappiness with his career -- would be ever be promoted? Should he look for a new opportunity? -- I thought it was a general malaise. And maybe it was all of those things, but what he said to me was, "Kimberly, what do you think about opening our relationship?" I had stared at him, my face metaphorically smashed against the windshield, and lost all my color. I became a black and white still shot. I choked out a "What?" and he started speaking rapidly about needing something different than what we had. "I love you," he said somewhere in there, and I believed him, but I also *couldn't fucking believe him.*

"You want to sleep with other people?" I asked, my breath shallow.

"I want to be able to love other people," he corrected calmly.

A rush of fear filled my entire gut and my eyes grew big. "You met someone," I said.

He didn't need to answer. I knew the answer already. I collapsed my chin against my chest and stopped breathing for what seemed like a long enough time for me to die, but I didn't, so I looked up at him and said, "I want to share my life with someone who wants to be in love me, not me and other people."

It wasn't our last conversation, but it was the most concise, the most relevant, the most controlled one we had as I packed a bag and moved in with my uptight cousin Rachel who I would be sure never to tell the real reason Jon and I split. Luckily, she hadn't asked too many questions when I'd called her to say I would love to rent the spare room in her apartment. She'd just told me to use my key and come when I wanted to. Jon and I hadn't figured out how we were splitting up our joint belongings yet. The very thought of doing that depressed me almost more than anything else -- that was the physicality of Jon and me -- our concrete presence in the world, soon to be divided and parceled out. Maybe I'd let him keep everything.

Only a handful of our friends knew about the split so far and most of them were pretty convinced we'd patch things up. I mean, never say never, but to me, when the man you love tells you he needs more than you, that spells *fini*. It tells me he doesn't have the balls to break up with me. That agreeing to take that step with him would mean sacrificing everything I held sacred in love and that my sacrifice would be answered with bitter disappointment when it turned out not to be *just a phase*, something our mutual friend Marla said to me over coffee yesterday afternoon.

Coffee, I needed something a little more dulling, not something so brightening. I needed to play Eights at Celia's party.

Eights, in case you didn't know, is a drinking game that involves a full deck of cards with the eight in every suite placed in the middle of the players. The rest of the cards are dealt evenly. Then the person left of the dealer will play either a seven or a nine (or as many cards as he has that go in sequence) of the same suite off the appropriate card and then assign drinks to the other players based on how many cards are on the table. So, for instance, if I have the nine, Jack, and Queen of Hearts, I play those off of the eight of hearts and then have four drinks to assign. I can divide them up, I can take them myself, I can do whatever I want with them.

It is very easy for every player to get wasted with this game.

Arriving at Celia's, I was Facebook-officially single and overwhelmingly sad, so, yeah, I got a little adolescent. And every time someone asked me about Jon -- whether they'd seen the Facebook change or not -- I felt my stomach pinch and the depth of my pain drop another league in the cliché sea of despair. So when Eights was over, I switched from beer to Bushmills on the rocks and found myself sitting in Celia's backyard alone at three forty-five in the morning. Most of the party-goers had either hit the road or passed out on the floor somewhere, but not me.

And not Todd.

Todd is one of my closest friends. Before I'd met Jon, Todd was rumored to be vying for my attention, something unconfirmed and unrealized.

Now Todd was Celia's boyfriend.

Celia had long ago gone to bed -- *"Too many Eights,"* she'd groaned on her way into her room -- and Todd had taken over host duties, even though he was not one of the four roommates, all of whom had gotten drunk quickly and therefore lost host credibility. Somehow Todd found me out there, sitting on their back stoop, staring at the empty grass.

"How's your night?" Todd asked, sitting down beside me and knocking the bottom of his beer bottle against my glass.

I shrugged and tried to see straight.

"Sorry to hear things are kinda shitty with Jon," Todd said.

"Things aren't shitty with him. They're over," I said bitterly.

Todd nodded. "Yeah, I might have heard something about that," he said.

I drew in some air. "And it sucks," I said.

Inside, Celia's iTunes played the Damien Rice version of the U2 song "One." It was slow and haunting. It stood out like an anthem. Todd and I sat and listened.

Is it getting better? / Or do you feel the same? / Will it make it easier on you now? / You got someone to blame / You say / One love / One life / When it's one need / In the night / One love / We get to share it...

Something cruel stirred inside of me, something that bubbled life to the surface. I set my glass down and got to my feet. Stretching my hand out towards Todd, I said in a flat voice, "Dance with me?"

Did I disappoint you? / Or leave a bad taste in your mouth? / You act like you never had love / And you want me to go without / Well it's / Too late / Tonight / To drag the past out into the light / We're one, but we're not the same / We get to / Carry each other / Carry each other...

Pressed against Todd's chest, my arms wrapped around his neck, his wrapped comfortably around my waist, I realized I was crying, truly crying, like I hadn't yet been able. A deep sob escaped my throat and I buried my face in his shoulder as his grasp tightened around me.

You say / Love is a temple / Love the higher law / You ask me to enter / But then you make me crawl / And I can't be holding on / To what you got / When all you got is hurt...

I felt at home in this moment, this pain paired with bliss, this comfort mated with complex sorrow. My hands crept up his neck and teased through his short, curly black hair as his hands dropped lower until they hugged just around my ass. I could feel the electricity running through our shared body, our connection as real as the ground beneath our feet or the stars hidden in the clouds overhead. Drawing my face away from his shoulder, I looked up to find him already looking down at me, only a slight tilt of the head necessary, and then the distance between us disappeared as he sank his kiss into me, warm and full, and leading to more of the same. I loved the feel of his lips against mine, his tongue in my mouth. I felt hungry for it, carried away, free. Todd was the one who broke us apart, who came to his senses first.

"I'm sorry," he said, stumbling back a step.

I stepped towards him. "Don't be," I said.

We stood close to each other, so close, but no longer touching. The moment still shimmered, even as reality crashed around us.

I was no better than Jon. I sat down in the grass.

Todd stood over me for a few hesitant moments before turning back towards the house. "Are you sleepinh here?" he asked thickly.

Head bowed, I tried to hear what he was really saying. Looking back towards him, I shook my head. I checked in with reality. We were at his girlfriend's house. He was not implying that we hook up in his girlfriend's house.

"I'm staying at my cousin's. She lives two blocks from here. I'll go home," I said softly.

Todd nodded slowly. "Be well, Kimberly," he said in an unreadable tone.

My head swimming, I climbed to my feet. "I'm glad you stopped that," I said, my voice still flat as I swigged my remaining whiskey. Wrapping my arms around him, I whispered in his ear, "I would have totally fucked you right here on the grass. And that would have lost us both everything."

I didn't look back as I walked away, but I heard the door close behind him as he made his way inside, surely to crawl into bed with the woman he loved.

I threw up once on the walk home and once again when I made it inside where I slept fitfully until the dawn that brought me out here to the porch, vowing never to drink again. Picking up my phone, I sent Celia a text that read *Fun party*, set the ringer to silent, and went back to staring at the hazy line of the sky.

First line by Sean OhEigeartaigh

Keys Open Doors

"Where the hell are my keys?"

"That sounds like an existential question if I ever heard one."

Dominic rolled his eyes as he patted the pockets of his winter coat. "Kayla, you're such a comedian," he muttered.

"Yes," she said lightly. "You know, earlier this afternoon, I was writing a poem about skeleton keys as both a physical and symbolic thing and now here I am, with you, who has lost, what was it? Oh yes, your keys. What do keys do? They unlock, they open. Or they lock, they close. They are the guardians of barriers -- they are soldiers, they are defense. And when that defense is lost, missing, gone rogue, what is it then?"

"An existential question," Dominic sighed. "But I really don't know where my keys are."

"Should've put them in a safe place, I guess," Kayla said, leaning against a brick wall. Behind that wall was a bar and in that bar were dozens of their friends celebrating a thirtieth birthday. They had slipped out of the party, though, in favor of quieter end of the night with a more exclusive guest list, but now their getaway was being thwarted.

"I probably left them on the bar," Dominic said, still patting his jacket.

It was Kayla's turn to sigh. "Want me to wait out here so people think I left already or do you think you'll get roped into another drink if you go in?"

Dominic stared at her for a moment and then said, "Wait here" as he made his way back inside. Maybe this key thing would work out to their advantage after all.

Dominic and Kayla used to date and then they broke up and then they became friends and then they became occasional friends-with-benefits and now they were an ambiguous mess that no one seemed to get. Kayla referred to Dominic as her *euphemism*; Dominic referred to Kayla as his *buddy*. Both of them slept with other people but kept winding back up on each other's doorstep, something Kayla's live-in boyfriend had taken recent issue with and kicked her out. Standing outside of the bar, she thought about the irony that she did have keys in her pocket, but they didn't unlock anything anymore.

Moments later, Dominic returned, triumphant, spinning his key ring around his finger. "Scored," he said. "Did anyone see you waiting out here?"

"Do you know how many people asked me tonight if I was staying with you since Bradley kicked me out?" Kayla said in lieu of answering his question.

"My guess is everyone asked you that -- because they asked me, too. Let's get in the car," he said, breathing out and creating a fog.

Kayla walked slowly around the passenger side door. "Yeah, everyone asked," she said.

"And did you stick with the story?" he asked, starting the engine.

"You mean, did I say, 'Hey, look over there?' and then run away?" Kayla asked with a smirk.

Dominic chuckled. "Yeah."

"Yeah," she said, staring straight out the slightly fogged windshield.

If she'd been forced to lie, she would have claimed she was staying with her sister who just happened to live in the same building as Dominic, a convenience that was usually how they'd start sleeping together again at the most unpredictable of moments. Kayla had actually really liked Bradley, for instance, maybe even loved him, but all it took was one late night encounter on the stairs for Dominic to seduce her back into his bed. Kayla didn't blame Bradley for dumping her -- she'd've done the same thing. It's actually why she broke up with Dominic in the first place -- she had no tolerance for cheaters. The fact that she *was* one now weighed upon her heavily and she wondered all the time if the influence Dominic had over her wasn't more damning than it was worth.

She'd have to think about that after they had sex, though. She wasn't ready to give *that* up quite yet.

Dominic parked his car in the lot by his building and they both got out and hurried inside. The temperature seemed to have dropped in the five minute drive. Kayla stopped him in the building's brightly lit lobby and kissed him.

"What was that for?" he asked, finally pulling back and grinning at her.

"Keys open doors," she said with a shrug, slinging her arm around his waist.

He lived in a studio apartment on the third floor so they hoofed it up the steps in tandem. Even though he was a foot taller than her, he slowed his gait to match hers and they made a game of this tiresome ascent. By the time they got to his door, they were both red faced and out of breath. He pulled his key out of his pocket and held it up for her to see.

"What is the meaning of this?" he asked, lowering it down and sliding it smoothly into the lock.

She grinned as he turned the knob and the door opened, revealing his pitch black apartment. "It's like a glimpse into your very soul," she said softly.

They kicked off their shoes and coats at the door and then closed it behind them, leaving them solidly in the dark. They didn't need light to find each other, though. They drew together, even in the absence of light of any kind, though they did stumble over wayward shoes and knock into a table before crashing together onto his unmade bed. Every night they spent together was intense and magnetic, like it could change her very molecular composition. This night was no different, only now she imagined herself as the lock and he was the key turning inside of her. But after the climax, he rolled away and she was left wondering -- was she now open or closed -- accessible or blocked -- defended or defenseless? She turned on the bedside lamp.

"How many women are you sleeping with these days?" she asked, sitting up.

He blinked at her, his face shifting from mellow to confused. "Why do you ask?"

"I just wanted to know," she said.

"I used a condom," he said.

"That's not what I asked," she said, her voice struggling to sound casual.

"Three," he said with a sigh, shifting his gaze up towards the ceiling. "But none of them are serious threats."

Kayla did a double take. "Serious threats?"

"Well, yeah, none of them are girlfriend material," Dominic said.

"So is that three including me or is it three women besides me?"

"Besides you," he said evasively. "Look, can we talk about something else?" He reached over and kissed the back of her hand. "Like, maybe what a great entrance we made at this private party?"

"Am I a serious threat?" she asked, ignoring his flirt.

Dominic sat up turned her to face him. "You're Kayla," he said simply.

"What does that mean?" she asked.

"It means... It means you're the best I've got," he said.

"But I'm not girlfriend material," she said.

Dominic rubbed his face with a flat palm. "That's not what I said."

"It's kind of what you said," Kayla pressed.

"Listen, can we talk about something else?" Dominic asked.

She studied his face and swallowed hard. "Maybe I should go stay at my sister's."

"Kayla, babe, it's nearly two in the morning. Your sister's gotta be sleeping by now. Stay put. Relax," Dominic said, kissing her on the forehead.

"I bet you say that to all the girls," she said dryly.

Dominic leaned back against the wall. "Where's this coming from?" he asked. "We've been who we've been for a long time now. Why so many questions all of the sudden?"

She shrugged and leaned against his chest. "I dunno, you lost your keys," she said.

He chuckled and put his arm around her. "Kayla, some days I wish I could see life through your eyes for even just an hour. It would change me profoundly."

"Doesn't just being around me change you profoundly?" she pouted.

"Well, yes. But having the chance to *be* you would be amazing." A pause. "You really need to stop asking existential questions about you and me." His voice had adopted a gentle edge.

"Why?" she asked.

"Because this is who we are. You're a great girl -- the best girl -- you're my standard. I covered a little earlier when I said those other girls weren't a serious threat -- I meant, they weren't a serious threat to outrank you."

"But," she said.

"But I'm not looking for a girlfriend. I'm not. If I was, you'd be it. But it's not what I want. I'm not a good boyfriend -- you know that, we've danced this dance. And what we have now is just better."

"It's safer," she said quietly. "Being committed to each other is scarier -- more dangerous -- it's leaving the door unlocked and being confident that the right people will gain access at the right time." She paused. "I had a really good thing with Bradley, you know? And I gave it up on a whim and for what?"

Dominic's breath was steady and even. "You knew exactly what you gave it up for."

She leaned over and turned off the bedside light and then stretched out long on her side of the bed. "Yeah," she said.

He mirrored her and turned his head on the pillow to face her. "I'm sorry I forgot my keys," he murmured.

Her expression remained flat in the darkness. "It's just semantics anyway," she said.

First line by Tom Lada

Sobriety

As she opened the refrigerator door, eight suicidal eggs jumped to their messy death. For a moment, she just stood there, a tad stunned. How the hell did that even happen? She was hung over and dehydrated and in severe need of scrambled eggs, but, Universe, not like this! Her eyes lingered on the devastation for another few moments before she simply closed the refrigerator door and walked away. Her sobriety level was at about thirteen percent. Shower, she needed a shower.

She got in the shower. Groggily, she applied shampoo and conditioner and soap to her body, rinsed, and repeated. Did the cleansing make her feel better? Was she really cleansed? Her mouth felt like it was full of cotton balls and steadiness was still a goal she hoped to achieve in the near future.

"I am definitely still drunk," she said out loud to her steamed up image in the bathroom mirror.

Wrapped in a towel, she padded back down the hallway to her bedroom. For a moment, she stood awkwardly outside and then knocked. It seemed absurd, but this was one morning where it felt absolutely necessary.

"Come in?" said a muffled voice.

She felt another five percent of sobriety creep up her spine as she timidly pushed the door open. The warm light of this early spring morning cascaded softly over the nearly naked body of her best friend Chad. He was face down on one of her pillows, his arms and legs akimbo. She took a moment to study him, the relaxed nature of his entire being. She had a friend who used the term *blissed out* on a regular basis and she felt like she was understanding its meaning for the first time in her life. This man was at home in her bed. Her degree of sobriety increased another ten percent.

She stood uncomfortably in the middle of her bedroom with the towel wrapped carelessly around her still damp body. Pursing her lips, she realized she had no idea what to do now.

"So..." she said lightly.

Chad turned his head and peeked up at her. She could see half of his smile, one of his dark brown eyes, and all of his curly black hair. She could also see his bare ass. It was right there.

"So..." he echoed, not moving any further.

She clutched her towel closer to her and cleared her throat. "There aren't any eggs," she said almost defensively.

His body shook as he chuckled. Lifting himself up and flipping around to face her, he grinned. She let her eyes fall on his Hanson t-shirt, worn only semi-ironically, and groaned inwardly. She had just had sex repeatedly with a man wearing a Hanson t-shirt.

Even worse -- she had just had sex repeatedly with *Chad*.

"Oh god," she groaned, readjusting her grip on her towel.

He patted the bed beside him. "Take a load off, Megan," he said.

"Could you put some underwear on?" she asked weakly.

It was as if Chad suddenly figured out why she was acting so weird. "Sure," he said slowly, leaning over to grab his boxers off the floor.

Once he was less exposed, she was less afraid of him, so she accepted his offer to sit down on the edge of her own bed. "So..." she repeated.

He leaned back against the head of her bed and studied her for a moment. "You OK?" he asked, genuine concern in his voice.

She shrugged. "Honestly, I don't know." Her sobriety level had gone up another twenty-two percent in the last few minutes and she was feeling less swimmy and more *oh shit*. She could tell that he had figured that out. She couldn't tell how he was feeling, so she asked. "You?"

His arms lay flat on the bed beside him and his eyes exuded the brightness of a man who was not completely destroyed by alcohol. "Good," he said simply.

"Good," she repeated. She didn't know what else to say.

"So there are no eggs?" he said.

She shook her head. "They all broke," she said.

"Well.... that's a good way to make eggs..." Chad said.

"No, I mean they broke on the floor," she said.

Chad raised his eyebrows in amusement. "Really? How did that happen?"

She shrugged. "I opened the door and they fell out," she said. "In fact, they're still on the floor."

He laughed at that one. "Seriously? It's not like you to leave a mess like that."

She stared at the floor where the rest of his clothes lay in a frantic heap. "Well, maybe I'm not myself at the moment."

His gaze followed hers and he cleared his throat. "Maybe," he repeated. Then his gaze shifted to her in her slouchy bath towel get up.

She watched his brain work.

"I'm feeling very naked under this towel," she said, a weak attempt at humor. "Can I have the room for a minute?"

"Sure," Chad said, sliding off her bed and padding down the hallway towards the bathroom.

She considered asking him to put on his pants, but, well, it was too late for that. Dropping her towel on the floor besides his abandoned clothes, she realized it was too late for a lot of things. She dressed quickly in a pair of jeans and a plain green t-shirt and let her damp hair frizz up around her as it dried. Opening the door, she heard him fussing around in the kitchen so she headed in that direction. Standing in the doorframe, she couldn't help but smile as she saw this half dressed man on his hands and knees scooping egg yolks and shells off the floor.

"Thanks," she said, grabbing the spray mop to clean up whatever remained.

"No problem," he said, washing his hands in the sink.

Once the kitchen was back in order, they stood quietly on opposite sides of the room.

"So..." she said again.

In two swift strides, he was across the room with a hand on her face as he lightly kissed her on the lips. "So," he said, his eyes inches from her own.

Instinctively, she stepped back. "I just... I don't know," she said. "Could you maybe go put your pants on?"

He looked down at his bare legs. "Oh," he said. "Sure."

She followed him back to her room and tried to think of something productive to say -- of *anything* to say really. Her sobriety had increased another seven percent by the time she was watching him hop into his jeans.

"Do you want me to leave?" he asked.

His question panicked her because she had no idea how to answer it. When she didn't say anything for a few moments, he started to move past her and she grabbed his arm. "No," she said in a breathy voice. "We have to talk about this right now."

This. Even though she said it, the word *this* made her feel like she was about to have a seizure. *What* is *this*? She didn't know -- she hoped he would start talking first. Sitting back down on the bed with her feet curled up into her chest as she leaned against the backboard, she now patted the space next to her for him to sit down. He was obedient. He seemed to be so *in this moment*, it made her feel lightheaded. How was he so calm? Her eyes fluttered closed and she tried to make her heart stop pounding.

"So last night..." he said. "It was awesome."

She clenched her eyes closed and drew her knees a little bit closer to her chest.

"It was?" she squeaked.

"It was for me," he said frankly.

She forced herself to unclench. "It was for me, too," she said, almost reluctantly. "I mean, the sex was awesome."

He chuckled again. "But I snore really loudly so the rest wasn't awesome?" he concluded.

She shot him an unmistakable look. "You know that's not what I mean," she said.

"Yeah... Yeah, I know."

"Can I just tell you what I remember? I was really drunk, but I remember some things happening and I need you to confirm them," she said, reaching a hand out and putting it on his forearm.

"OK," he said.

"I remember you offering to walk me home from the bar. I remember us standing outside talking for awhile..." She hesitated. "I remember you saying you were in love with me," she continued, her voice now barely a whisper.

He nodded a confirmation and said nothing.

So she went on. "I remember you saying you were in love with me and kissing me and asking if you could come in and I wasn't sure but I finally said OK. And once we were inside..."

"We ripped each other's clothes off pretty fucking fast," Chad inserted.

"Did you use a condom?" she asked.

He nodded. "Every time," he confirmed.

"Oh, good," she exhaled. She felt a bit more relaxed now that the facts were on the table. "God, Chad, I never thought this would happen between us."

He looked surprised. "Really? Never?"

"Well, we've been friends for so long and there's never been anything beyond that..." she said.

"You haven't been paying attention, I guess," he said quietly. "I've loved you for a very long time."

Her discomfort set back in. She could not say the same thing back to him. To ease her unease, she asked, "Was this your plan when you offered to walk me home?"

He shook his head and stared at his fingernails. She knew he was resisting the urge to chew on them. "No, I guess I was drunk enough and the stars had aligned the right way above us outside your apartment..."

She studied his profile and felt such a deep bond with him at that moment -- was it love? Did she love him? She shook the thought off and knew it wasn't a question she needed to tackle today. There were bigger issues -- bigger problems -- worse than broken eggs on her kitchen floor -- and they would need to be addressed first. She could feel he was gearing up towards a big speech, a confession, a heart-bending tribute to his feelings for her, but she had sat through as much of that this morning as she was ready to handle. Before he could continue talking, she flipped herself over him, straddling his legs, and kissed him passionately. It tasted bitter and vaguely of whiskey and it stirred something inside of her that made her feel instantly guilty and empowered. He pressed his hands into her and she scooped her fingers through his curls.

"I think I have one condom left," he managed to say.

She didn't respond verbally but instead pulled her shirt over her head. She hadn't bothered to put on a bra. She laid back on the bed and let him run his hands and his mouth over her. Her degree of sobriety was now at a full ninety-seven percent. She felt wicked and ready to be destroyed.

And then she was destroyed. Her cell phone was ringing -- it was "Benny and the Jets" -- it was Olivia.

"Shit," she said, her breath heaving.

Chad froze above her as they both listened to the ring tone. "My battery's dead," he mumbled.

She nodded and scrambled up. Closing her eyes, she answered the phone. "Hey, Liv," she said.

"Meggie! Have you seen Chad? He never came home last night..." Olivia said. "And I think his cell's dead. I've been trying it all night. You were out with him, though, right?"

"Yeah," she said with forced lightness. "He crashed here. He's here."

"Oh, OK, awesome! I was so worried something happened to him. Can I talk to him for a quick second?" Olivia asked brightly.

"Sure," she said tiredly. Her sobriety was now at one hundred percent. "Your girlfriend," she added succinctly, handing Chad the phone.

"Hey Liv," Chad said.

She slid on her shirt as she got up and left him alone in the room. In so many ways, she wished they hadn't already cleaned up the kitchen. At that moment, all she wanted to do was crawl on her kitchen floor and make jokes in her head that began, *"In order to make an omelet..."* Instead, she flipped on the coffee pot and stared at a magnet on her refrigerator that said: *The only true happiness is to love and to be loved.*

A few minutes later, Chad came into the kitchen, fully dressed once more. "I should probably go," he said, avoiding her eye contact for the first time all morning.

"Reality bites," she said with a shrug.

He walked over and embraced her tightly, with a confidence she couldn't quite interpret. "We'll figure this out," he said. "But I've got to deal with Olivia first."

"Right... First," she said, squeezing him back and trying to lift the irony out of her voice.

"I'll call you later," he said, letting her go.

"Once your phone's charged," she said.

"Yeah," he said. As he turned to open the door, he looked back at her and said, "I really did have fun."

"Me, too," she said.

When the door closed behind him, she sank to the floor and stared at the spot where the egg catastrophe had cracked her morning wide open. She appreciated a good metaphor, Universe.

Her sobriety was now at one hundred and ten percent and climbing.

First line by Tina Miller

The Way You Looked at Me

I will never, in my life, forget the way you looked at me on the sidewalk that late night in January. The light snow floating through a beam of street light, a car zooming by, and us. You were talking -- I remember your lips moving -- I remember sound coming out -- but I don't know what you were saying. I was too fixed -- too stunned -- too captivated by the severity of your stare, the depth of it, the completeness of its intent. You must have been saying goodbye. You must have been explaining why. I stood with my arms folded in an X across my chest, gloved fingers grasping tightly onto opposite shoulders. I wanted to look away, but I didn't. I couldn't. Your sheer force of earnestness kept me locked in this moment, no escaping, no changing this outcome. I didn't hear what you said, true, but it turned out I didn't need to hear -- being able to see was more than enough. Being able to suspend my reality in the breath of the moment it took for your gaze to swallow me whole turned out to be the culmination of my fear. You would break that gaze any moment -- you would lift your foot carefully and pivot -- you would slowly and assuredly walk away. And I would stand still for a very long time, my hands still crossing my chest, unblinking as the snow found a temporary home on the tips of my eyelashes before melting away forever.

First line by Shannon Robinson

Dinner for One

If there was a taco worth taking a bite of, *this* was that taco. The red snapper was perfectly sautéed with garlic, butter, and lime juice and housed snugly in a crisp, corn taco shell finished off with sour cream, spicy cheese, a few jalapeños, a tuft of bright green lettuce, and, the best part -- my very own hot sauce. On the side, I had a fresh bowl of the second best part -- my homemade seven layer dip, starring my world famous guacamole, and a bowl of tortilla chips, hot and salty, purchased twenty minutes ago at the fancy Mexican restaurant down the hill from my condo. In my glass, I'd just poured the avocado margarita I'd whipped up with the extras not used in the guacamole. And when all of that was said and done, fried ice cream for dessert. My eyes danced over the plate before me, out here on my back porch overlooking the Boston Harbor. I'd turned on the white Christmas lights I kept strung around the wooden posts and lit a single unscented candle and laid my linen napkin across my lap before I took the first mouth-watering bite. I closed my eyes as I cracked through the shell. It was everything I dreamed it could be. And more. Savoring it for as long as possible, I took my time chewing and swallowing and waited a moment even longer before opening my eyes.

The only thing this scene lacked was a companion to turn to and say, "Holy shit, that is good."

So I ate the pair of tacos in silence, save the light sounds of my Pandora riffing off of my Marcus Anthony selection, and then scooped into the seven layer dip with the savory tortilla chips, all the while keeping my margarita glass full to the top, just adding tequila when the avocado mix ran out. The meal was delectable, and when I finally remembered I had fried ice cream as well, I enjoyed that, too. By the time the last mouthful was consumed, I was drunk enough not to notice that mine was the only chair at this table, that I'd taken away the one that used to belong to Stacey. I never allowed anyone else to come over, not ever, and now with the way things were, I doubted I'd ever let anyone else come into my home again.

I got up from the table and carried my dishes into the kitchen in an unstable stack, setting them precariously close to the edge of the sink. If I would have stepped too aggressively on the hardwood floor, the whole pile would have clattered to the ground and resulted in shards of unfixable dishware, and I had such nice dishware -- Fiesta plates in marigold, cobalt, and paprika with mixed-and-matched glassware, including sixteen-ounce Cooler glasses, clear with vibrant stripes. That's what I'd used for my margarita glassware, despite the fact that I had very nice margarita glasses. They were only fourteen-ounces, though, so I went for the bang-for-your-buck advantage of the Coolers tonight. And now all my careful planning was sucked down the drain along with an empty bottle of 1800 silver. Why didn't I just use the regular Cuervo for my cocktails? My life would not be in such a state of immediate chaos if I'd planned more responsibly.

Once I'd cleared all of the plates from the porch, I did take a moment to slide the tower of dishes more squarely on the marble counter before I started washing them. My Pandora station was playing "Waiting for Tonight" by Ms. Jennifer Lopez and I belted that out while I turned the water to scalding and slid rinsed dish after rinsed dish into the dishwasher, dancing a little as I went along. My hands turned a bright, blistery red, but I didn't feel any pain. No, there was no pain in this old body. Ms. Lopez and I continued our duet -- *Gone are the days when the sun used to set on my empty heart all alone in my bed. Tossing and turning, emotions were strong -- I knew I had to hold on, waiting for tonight, when you would be here in my arms...* I did not recognize the irony of the lyrics in that moment, I will confess, but once the song switched to one I could not belt because it was in Spanish, a language I did not speak, my mouth continued to hum the previous song and it was then that I realized I was the opposite of Ms. Jennifer Lopez. In every way possible.

I fell to my knees in the middle of my kitchen. I watched the steam rise out of the sink as the blazingly hot water continued to stream out. I stared at my red hands and I started to cry. My chin dragged down against my chest and the tears lobbed themselves out of my eyes and onto my white linen shirt and my blue silk tie. I was destroying everything tonight, it seemed.

But then a thunder rose deep inside of me and pulled me back to my feet and stopped my tears. I turned off the water, turned on the dishwasher, and stormed through the white and black of my apartment until I found my iPhone, tucked in my briefcase still. Withdrawing it, I dialed Stacey's number and it rang three times before she answered.

"Luther?" she said, referring to me, as always, by my last name.

"Stacey, I needed to say something to you. I am very drunk," I said.

There was a pause. "Rum-drunk or whiskey-drunk?" she asked.

Clever lady. She knew that when I drank rum I got loud and sappy and when I drank whiskey I got quiet and mean.

"Tequila," I bristled. "None of your business."

"Oh," she said.

Delighted to have confused her, I went on. "What's to be said in this moment is I ate a delicious meal of food tonight made of fish tacos and seven-layered chip dip and also some green-colored margaritas and I ate it alone because you failed me."

"I *failed* you?" Stacey repeated.

"Yes, are you misunderstanding me already?" I sputtered. "You could have been here having this feast with me on my nice dishes and dancing around to Ms. Jennifer Lopez' singy-things with me but, no, no, you couldn't because you universally suck."

"Luther, are you OK? Should I come over? I'm coming over," Stacey said, her voice pitched.

"Noooooooooooooooooo," I mooed. "You are not allowed in my domain. I will not grant you access to the elevator so don't come over. That's the point -- you blew it, missy."

"What are you talking about?" she asked.

"Where are you right now? Are you with *Marcus* from *work*?" I asked. "Are you at that stupid stupid dumb *pub* you always go to with *Marcus* from *work*?"

"Ummm..." Stacey began.

"I knew it. I knew that's where you were, gypsy lady. Don't come here. I won't let you unzip anything on me, so there's no point. This is my castle and I don't let people in here," I said.

"Luther. We've been over this. You know Marcus is married with four kids. He's just a colleague. And for the record, he's not here right now..."

"He's got one of those *open* marriages though, I bet. The kind where you have sex with everyone and it doesn't matter if they've got someone who loves them a lot because it's the only way to get to have sex with everyone is to have it all *open* like that," I said, my voice starting to lose some steam.

"I don't think Marcus's got an open marriage..." Stacey said.

"Well, be fucking happy with him anyway," I said. "Because I can't let you come up here anymore."

"Luther, what the hell is going on?" Stacey asked.

"You didn't RSVP to the party," I said.

There was a long pause. "What party?"

"The party I invited you to at my co-worker's house next weekend. You didn't RSVP," I hiccuped.

"Luther, I told you I could go," Stacey said slowly.

"Yes, but you didn't RSVP. It's really important that you RSVP so the host knows how many people are coming and you didn't do that. It's not my job to RSVP *for* you. You got your own invitation and you're a rude stupid gypsy for not RSVP-ing," I said, my voice gaining momentum once more. "I can't be with someone who has no manners or respect for people hosting parties."

There was the longest pause yet. "Wait, are you breaking up with me?" she asked.

"I already broke up with you in my mind because you suck at being polite so I guess this is the formal announcement, yes," I said. "Why else would I not invite you over for the most amazing fish taco dinner of my life, you dumb gypsy?"

"Luther, I think we should talk about this when you're sober. I'll call you tomorrow," she said, hanging up.

I stared at the phone until the screen snapped to black. "Tequila-sober!" I yelled at no one.

I kicked off my shoes and bumbled out of my clothes before slipping on my favorite pair of silk pajamas and curling up in bed with my white fluffy stuffed dog named Dr. Porkchop. Not even when I would speak with Stacey the next day and she would explain my margarita-rant would I fully understand most of what she said.

But I would confirm that she was dumped because she had no fucking manners. That much would hold true from the solo dinner party confession. I mean, how hard is it to RSVP? I was quite sure she'd never make that mistake again. I did, however, think of her every time I made fish tacos alone.

First line by Bill Anderson

Friends

"I mean, how many chaturangas can one gal do?"

Berrie lolled her head towards Ginny's voice and frowned. Ginny's pronunciation of the Sanskrit term for *yoga pushup* sounded like *chat-u-granda*. Awful. "There are, like, ninety in this class. I told you that going in."

"But you didn't really," Ginny whined, tailing after Berrie towards the Starbucks across the street from Namaste Yoga. "You didn't really tell me at all."

Berrie stopped in the middle of the crosswalk and turned to face her accuser. "Seriously, Gin?"

Ginny's face paled as cars slammed on their brakes and horns honked. "Seriously?" she squeaked.

Berrie let out an exasperated sigh and spun around on her heels to continue towards her well-deserved iced coconut mocha. "Bullshit," she said.

Ginny followed her into the coffee shop like a scared rabbit. "You said that I'd be able to keep up."

"*You* said you'd done yoga before. In fact, I believe your exact quote was, 'Berrie, Berrie, please please let me come to yoga with you! I've been doing yoga all my life and it would be so so fun!'" Berrie did an awesome Ginny impression. Awesome enough to turn Ginny's face bright red.

"I don't sound like that," she said. "And, well, I *have* done yoga before." Insert dramatic pause to give Berrie a moment to recall her use of the word *chaturanga*. "Just nothing like *that*."

Berrie tried to mask her pleasure in this moment. "Astanga is the *only kind of yoga*! Primary Series is the best practice to do!" she barked in a voice loud enough to be authoritative without yelling.

Ginny's eyes couldn't possibly grow any rounder, yet look at that -- rounder. "I thought we'd be doing some stretching..." she said meekly.

Berrie snorted. "Well, we did plenty of that."

"Yes, but it was so *hard*. And there was so much *Sanskrit*. I think the only thing I knew how to do really was a Sun A and after that, I was totally lost!"

Truth be told, Berrie was somewhat lost during class as well. She actually had never gone to a Primary Series class before, largely because it seemed too hard and had too many vinyasas -- which involved the *chaturangas* Ginny had started complaining about two-point-two seconds after they'd left the studio -- but she'd faked her way through as if she'd been doing this specific practice since the day she was born, thanking god for her inflamed competitive gene with every forward fold.

"You know, you didn't have to do all of the vinyasas," Berrie said in a snotty voice. "You could have skipped some if they were too hard."

Ginny laughed in a short burst. "Those were the only things I really knew how to do though!! Why didn't you tell me..."

Berrie held up a hand in Ginny's face. "I'll have a venti iced coconut mocha, light on the ice, heavy on the mocha," she ordered as she handed the cashier her debit card. Taking her hand back down, she maintained a humorless expression as she said, "Listen, Ginny, you're, what four months younger than me? You should be a little more adaptable to this. How else will things ever last between you and my dad?" Now, insert the brightest smile possible on Berrie's face.

Ginny ordered a tall iced coffee and frowned. "What does that mean?"

Berrie shrugged. "I mean... You can't even keep up with my dad's youngest kid -- wait'll you try and hang with my older sisters. Alysia is a rock climber and Allyson has run three marathons. I'm assuming you'll want to try and be just like them and pretend to be an expert at what they love to do to weasel your way in, am I right?"

Ginny blushed. "I love your father," she mumbled.

Berrie patted her arm sympathetically. "He's a lovable guy," she said. "But he likes truly ambitious women, not meddling copycat wanna-be's." Her voice was singsong, as if Ginny was actually a four-year-old wearing a paper crown and declaring herself the Queen of England.

Ginny swallowed hard and her jaw clenched. "All I wanted to be was your friend."

"Venti iced coconut mocha!" the barrista called.

Berrie grabbed her drink off the counter and smiled at Ginny. "Well, *namaste.* Add me on Facebook then," she said smartly, stalking out the door.

First line by Karen Caiazzo

The Crawl

The only way I can make it through this pub crawl is with this flask in my pocket. It's full of Jamesons because I'm an unoriginal bastard. Before leaving the apartment this morning, my girlfriend, who is far too intelligent to join us on this annual time-suck, suggested I fill it with Dr. McGuillicuddy's menthol mint schnapps for a couple of reasons -- one, because we have a gigantic plastic bottle of it sitting uselessly on top of our refrigerator and two, because she thought it might serve nicely to *cleanse the pallet* over the course of the crawl. Ha, Cynthia, what a woman she is. Me, I ignored her muttering and filled my stainless steel flask with the only thing any respectable drunk puts into a flask -- whiskey. To the brim.

We're on the seventh bar now. It's a tight group this year, just seven of us. Seven at the seventh. Look at that. It's Lloyd, Gina, Beth, Todd, Robby, Carmen, and me. Back in the old days, there'd be twenty of us -- forty even -- at this stage of the day. But that's what happens when people get older and start having babies and marriages and responsibilities that bridge beyond get shitfaced on a Saturday afternoon. I guess Lloyd, Gina, Beth, Todd, Robby, Carmen, and I don't know a thing about that since we're getting shitfaced on a Saturday afternoon. This is a tradition started by Lloyd, Gina, and me, back when we were undergrads at UMass, legally able to drink and so we did -- a lot. *"What if we did this all day?"* Lloyd had postured. What if? So we did. The first crawl was back in 2002 and it was just the three of us. Gina and I used to fuck back then, even though Lloyd was head over heels for her. I don't know how he could stand the sight of us, let alone go from bar to bar, 10AM until 2AM, watching us all over each other. But he did it. He's quite something, that Lloyd. Anyway, he and Gina are married now, if you can believe it. The flask in my pocket was my best man's gift. It's got my name engraved on it and everything. And we're still doing this shit -- planning day-long drinking exploits. Gina and Lloyd are the only married people I know who don't need to spend their Saturdays at Bed Bath and Beyond or whatever.

Seventh bar, so it's a little after four in the afternoon. I look around at the crew, mostly the usual suspects, and feel a little depressed as I sneak a swig from my flask. Beth is here because she's Gina's bestie. Todd and Carmen are old college pals who joined us on the Second Annual Crawl and haven't missed one since. And Robby? He's either screwing Beth or a work-colleague of Lloyd's that Gina wants to set up with Beth. I didn't pay much attention to all of that. By this point in the day, it doesn't really matter. He's the token new guy. We get one every year. There's always one that we have to remind it's not a sprint, it's a marathon. Stick to one drink per bar and no shots and you'll do fine, kid. Trust us -- we're sage-like. I'm sitting on a bar stool a little ways away from the rest of the group and I'm staring at my untouched Bud Light. I fucking hate Bud Light, but, well, I ordered it so what am I really complaining about? It's like I'm trying to draw as much attention to my absolute misery as I am humanly capable of doing. Fuck you, Bud Light. I take a large gulp and, stone faced, take another.

The bartender is this guy Damien who plays in a band I like called Gutter Snipes. He's the singer. A little overly dramatic on stage, but the tunes are solid, so I forgive his Academy Award losing performances. When he saw our sorry selves roll in a few minutes ago, his entire face lit up like a goddamn Christmas tree. Could we really be anyone's highlight? I drum lightly on the flask in my pocket and wait for him to ask me where Cynthia is -- only he'll call her *Cindy*. It's a well-known fact that my boy Damien has a thing for *Cindy*.

"Say, man, where's Cindy?" Damien asks not two seconds later.

I appreciate how casual he tries to sound -- how bored, even. I take another swig from my Bud Light, draining half the bottle as I go.

"She's working today," I say. *On her abs*, I add silently, knowing she's probably at the gym deciding between yoga and spinning right about now.

"Oh, seriously? That's too bad. It's too nice a day to be working," he says.

"You're working," I say.

Damien blinks at me. "That's how I know it's too nice a day to be working," he says.

Whaaaaaaat a smartass. "True, man. At least you got us drunks to keep you company for a bit," I say.

Damien eyes the rest of the group -- everyone's gotten giggly for some reason all of the sudden -- and I can see that Christmas morning glory fading from his eyes. "What're you guys up to?" he asks. "Besides getting drunk."

I shrug. "Nothing. Just that."

"Oh," Damien says.

"Pub crawl," I add.

Here Damien's eyes flash once more. He'd been on the crawl with us maybe three or four years ago. That's when he'd met *Cindy*.

"Didn't know you guys still did that," he said.

I nod. "This is our tenth," I say.

Damien whistles through his teeth. "That's a lotta crawlin'."

"You're telling me," I say.

Damien walks away right about then to serve Robby who's finally made up his mind about what he wants to drink, and I take that opportunity to take a swig from my flask. Before I even have the lid on and the thing slid back in my pocket, Gina's by my side, twisting a yellow curl around her finger.

"Having fun?" she asks me.

She knows I'm not having fun, but I try to humor her. "I love drinking. I love drinking all day. I love drinking all day on pub crawl."

Gina sighs and sits down beside me. "Amanda's not coming," she says.

I freeze for a moment and then shake my head just a little. "So?" I say.

Gina folds her arms close to her chest and shrugs. "I thought you'd like to know. Maybe that would help your mood."

Here, I full on shake my head. "Why should I give a fuck if she's here or not?" I ask.

"Because I know you do," Gina said calmly. "I know you do."

"Well, you're wrong," I say. "I don't give a fuck."

"Sure," Gina sighs as she hops off the bar stool and returns to the people actually having a good time.

You're such a liar, says Amanda's voice, exploding in my head.

"So what?" I mutter.

So what, Amanda? So what if she usually would be here with us, part of the crew, but isn't and it's all because of me? I down the rest of my Bud Light in a single swallow and check my phone. There's a text from Cynthia. It says *Tell Damien Cindy says heeeeeey*. I smile at this. My girl's checking the schedule and she knows where I am. It matters to me that she cares, even if she's not here in person. She only ever came on the crawl once when we were first dating, likely to prove that she could hang with my crew, and after she earned her stripes, she never needed to do it again. I admire that about her. She's her own person who does what she needs to do to make herself the best she can be. Maybe that sounds corny -- maybe it *is* corny -- but I wish I was more like that. I thank god every day when I wake up and she's sleeping there beside me still. One of these days she's going to figure out she's way better than me, but every day she doesn't is a blessing.

Amanda, she figured me out. She figured me out a long time ago. She's one of those people who got absorbed into our group somehow along the way. I'm not even sure who hooked her in, but once she showed up, it was as if she'd always been there. I met her six months before I met Cynthia and I would be lying if I didn't admit Amanda and I had a kinda thing for each other that never amounted to more than one or two drunken make out sessions. Somehow, the timing for us to figure it out beyond that point just never synchronized. And then I met Cynthia -- and with Cynthia, everything worked out flawlessly. I'd never been in a relationship that was so easy. Everyone was thrilled and everyone was so crazy about Cynthia -- except, of course, for Amanda. Amanda was a good friend and I hoped we could work it out, and we did, for the most part. But I knew that she could see me for who I was -- an underachieving drunk with a good sense of humor -- and that made her dangerous for me. It made me respect her more because she was willing to tell me when I was being a dick. No one else ever did. She pointed out my good stuff, too, don't get me wrong, but there is nothing quite as valuable as a friend who you know will *always* tell you the truth. For me, that friend was Amanda.

A week ago, Amanda and I sat at The Burren, her favorite Somerville haunt, having some beers and catching up on life. She'd just split from this guy she'd been seeing for a few months -- a real pretentious hipster, in my opinion -- so she was drinking bourbon, straight up, and it was going right to her head. I was sympathy drinking right along with her and was likely the cooler of the two heads, but, whatever, a drunk person is a drunk person, and we were a pair of those for sure. Somehow the conversation turned a spotlight on my relationship with Cynthia and after a few moments of doe-eyed babbling from me, Amanda, in one of her more bitter moments, said, "And I never even got to fuck you." And then me, true to form drunken jokester, said, "We can go fuck right now if that will make you feel better." She stood up immediately and said, "It will. Let's go."

Well, we didn't go right at that moment. We had to close our tab, first. But then she dragged me out of the bar and down the street towards her nearby apartment. My legs were like jelly and my eyes darted around in an attempt to find focus. Amanda seemed confident, grasping tightly to my hand I guess so I couldn't escape. The whole thing was surreal. When we got to her apartment building, she fussed in her bag for the keys and I started to sway back and forth on the porch beside her. What was I doing here?

"Amanda, what am I doing here?" I said out loud.

She turned sharply and stared at me through narrowed eyes. "We're having sex tonight," she said flatly, yanking the door open and grabbing my hand once more.

But I didn't move. "I can't do that," I said.

Amanda didn't let go of my hand, but her grasp weakened. "Why?"

"You know why," I muttered. "I love my girlfriend."

She studied me carefully for a long, hard moment before slowly drawing the hand she held behind her back and bringing herself closer to me. Standing just a breath's distance from me face, she hovered her lips over mine. I would be lying if I said I didn't feel the heat between us, the chemistry. I would be lying if I said I didn't want her in that moment, want her more than almost any woman I'd ever wanted before. There was a paper thin distance separating us and it was more than my body could handle. I kissed her -- I did it. I kissed her with a rawness that I had never quite experienced before and she devoured me, right there on her porch.

"Come," she pleaded, breaking the kiss. "Come in."

I leaned my forehead against hers and drew my hands tight across her back. "I gotta go home," I said.

Amanda bit her lip and turned her face away from me. "I'll never understand you," she said.

"I'm sorry," I said.

"Yeah," she said, shaking out of my arms and disappearing into her building.

I walked home slowly that night, confused and stunned, and when I found Cynthia sprawled on the couch in a pair of my boxer shorts and a Beatles t-shirt, I felt a slow simmer in my gut -- it was a distinct mixture of lust and gratitude with a healthy over-seasoning of guilt.

"My, you're drunk," she said, smiling sweetly at me. "How's Amanda feeling about the breakup?"

I lunged onto the couch beside her and scooped her up in my arms. Kissing her deeply, I leaned my entire body weight onto her. "Hi," I said.

"Hi," she said.

And there was no more talk of Amanda that night.

Now it's a week later and Amanda's maybe pissed at me and I'm maybe pissed at her and I don't know who's heard what about what happened and I'm on this fucking pub crawl and I'm miserable. Gina, she clearly knows the whole story, and she's been kind and non-judgmental since she called me up two days after it happened to say, "So Amanda and you..."

"There is no *Amanda and me*," I'd said defensively.

"I know," Gina had said gently.

And if Cynthia ever found out, there'd be no *Cynthia and me*, either. I think about this as I re-read her text message -- *Tell Damien Cindy says heeeeeey.* I look at the time -- 4:30PM. Hopping off the bar stool, I walk over to the group and pull Gina aside.

"I'm gonna take off," I say.

Gina's eyes bug out. "What?"

"Yeah, I'm gonna go meet up with Cynthia, I think. Text Amanda and say it's all clear if she wants to come out with you guys."

Gina stammers. "OK."

I turn to the rest of the crew and offer a salute. "I'm outta here, guys," I say.

And before they can offer a word of protest, I'm out the door, my finger hitting *send* on Cynthia's number.

First line by Camilo Guaqueta

A New Soft Light

She could feel his heartbeat in the sole of her shoe. Even thinking that quietly to herself made her feel like an angsty teenager again. But, in a way, that's exactly what she was. Freshly in love, ready for the wind to be pleasantly knocked out of her on a daily basis. This was the wonder of it, this thing so long foreign to her senses. *Love. Love a thub-thub*, right there, beating in her shoe. Did that make them sole-mates? She made silent jokes like that to take the pressure off, to distract. She needed to be distracted. She didn't believe in love, hadn't for a long time, so how could she possibly be in it now?

A new soft light in her eyes told a different story. A less jaded one. A less broken one. She could love and she did and she was.

Six weeks ago, she sat alone in a coffee shop reading *The Girl with the Dragon Tattoo* because she refused to see the movie without turning every page first -- an irony, considering she was reading it on her Kindle, which gauged her progress through any given book by what percentage she'd read, not which page she was on, the same analogy applied. Until she got to the end of Blomkvist and Salander's fucked up adventure story, she would not buy a ticket, that was her rule. That was when she met him, as she sat there furiously reading.

"I like it better when people have the actual book," he'd said before she'd noticed him looking at her.

Her green eyes lifted from the screen and connected squarely with his brown ones. "Oh?" she'd said.

He'd nodded slightly, setting down his pencil on a sudoku puzzle. "Yeah, I can't tell what anyone's reading these days. Whatever you've got there has you looking ready to kill someone."

A slight blush rose in her cheeks. "Oh... Really? It's just *The Girl with the Dragon Tattoo...*"

"You're trying to finish it before the movie comes out?" he'd ventured.

She'd nodded and then nodded again when he'd asked if he could come and join her for a cup of coffee and nodded once more when he'd asked if he could have her number. Leaving the coffee shop later that evening, she'd braced herself against an early December chill that suddenly seemed less harsh.

She finished the book on opening day and for their fourth date, he took her to see the movie -- an experience that might have daunted an ordinary new couple given the graphic nature of sexual violence depicted in the film, but for them, it lead to an all-night discussion about love and recovery. No one was without his or her demons, even if they weren't necessarily made for the big screen and as the pink light of dawn rose on them, cuddled up on her couch, she felt her own rebirth happen with him there beside her. He was her chance to be whole again.

It took her awhile to admit this out loud, though. It took her awhile to admit that's what was actually happening to her. Her friends didn't say a word about the changes in her, and she was fairly certain this was because they were afraid to jinx it. They liked this guy, this affable guy who'd picked her up in a coffee shop. While the rest of them slaved through online dating, all she had to do was sit there and wait for this guy to notice her. Lucky girl. She felt lucky. She felt lucky every day.

She felt his heart beat in the soul of her foot. She felt him tucked away in her brain. She felt him become as a part of her as her very own cells.

Nothing -- nothing terrified her more.

"You know I'm not him," he'd say quietly when they'd lay in bed at night.

She'd feel her entire body seize with panic. "Who?" she'd ask.

"Him. Whoever didn't love you the right way."

She'd roll over to study his profile. "I know," she'd say, but her voice always trailed at the end, as if maybe it would forever be a question.

First line by Tina Miller

Blame

Every morning began with him saying, "I don't know who to blame." He'd look sideways out the East Window and let his gaze linger somewhere over the water while his nine-year-old daughter sat stoically across the table eating her cereal. He would cluck his tongue and lose track of the time for a spell before something would turn his head back to the sullen stare of his only child.

"Daddy, you're weird," she'd say if she said anything at all. Usually, though, she just sat silently and crunched on her cereal, spooning the extra milk into her mouth like cold soup.

On the mornings she stayed quiet, he would smile awkwardly at her, as if he suddenly realized she was in the room, and add something like, "The President, God, the economy, Hollywood, the public schools, the internet, rock-n-roll," and shake his head. He never did a good job at articulating his point.

"I miss Mama," his daughter would mutter as she rinsed out her bowl and placed it in the dishwasher.

He would watch her skulk out of the kitchen and then bury his head in his hands.

With the room to himself, he would trace his gaze back out the East Window and let it rest on the water once more. Sometimes his thoughts would become clearer once he had the room to himself. Having his daughter nearby caused him more anxiety than he would ever be willing to admit -- partly because she was looking at him with heavy judgement in her eyes and also partly because her eyes looked so much like her mother's, his wife, the only woman he would love in his entire long life. She'd died the previous summer from a disease that proved incurable and with her last breath went his, never again able to look into another human's eyes and feel understood, a severe frustration especially considering their daughter's eyes were so strikingly similar to her mother's.

When he'd met his wife, she was sitting alone in a food court at the mall and he was trying to walk through without making eye contact with anyone. But something about her physical being slowed him down and turned his head and he did what he never did -- he stopped. He sat down. He said, "I have a habit of not talking to strangers," to which she'd quipped, "Well, safety first."

It was like they'd known each other in past life, shared a history longer than their waking conscious could ever comprehend. It's the only explanation for why she gave him a chance, gave him her everything, gave him an offspring, gave him her last breath of air.

"Daddy, I'm leaving for the bus," his daughter would say most mornings before she'd dart out the door.

He'd barely respond. He'd stare out that window fixated on who to blame for nothing in particular and push a sigh out through his mouth.

First line by Holland Dieringer

Better Off Alone

My auntie always told me: when you feel like you really don't wanna be alone, you probably need to spend some time alone. I had her words pounding through my brain as I walked away from Jeremiah on Tuesday night, resisting the urge to draw my phone from my pocket and call Saul or Beanie to find out what they were doing. I mean, I knew what they were doing: Saul was stoned and drinking Coors Light at Marvel's listening to his friend Clever Joe play some ill-conceived reggae while Beanie was likely sitting at home, half in her pajamas, hoping I would call and give her an excuse to roll her eyes and say, "Mara, you are going to be the reason I hate tomorrow." Calling either of these people would make me hate tomorrow, too, so I left my phone in my pocket and trudged towards home. It was midnight, after all, on a Tuesday. Realistically, I should be headed for bed.

Jeremiah lived in a new apartment complex in Somerville about a ten minute walk from my own place. When he'd first moved there from East Boston, I'd been thrilled -- he'd be so much closer -- we could conveniently run into each other far more often, which we did, and that was nice. But I still felt the resistant distance between us, even living so much closer to each other, and I was no more ready now to call him my boyfriend than I was eleven months ago when we'd met at Fenway Park. On that night, I'd come dressed to impress -- short black mini skirt, bright green Red Sox tank top, pink Red Sox hat, and three-inch platform wedges. Beanie had failed to mention she'd purchased standing room only tickets so the night was proving to be more difficult than seemed necessary. At one point near the sixth inning, I'd excused myself from Beanie and our other friends to sit on the steps heading towards nearby concessions when a tall, lanky man dressed in Orioles gear sat down beside me.

"Not a big baseball fan?" he asked, not actually looking at me.

I was startled and turned to stare at his profile. "Beg pardon?"

"You've got a pink hat on," he said, his eyes only peeking towards me.

I placed a protective hand on my head. "Yeah, so?"

"So you're not a real baseball fan," he said. "Real baseball fans would never wear the pink hats. They're for girls who want to look like fans at the ballpark, but they really don't fool anyone."

My jaw gaped open in surprise, but I couldn't think of a decent comeback. Particularly because he was right -- I wasn't a baseball fan.

"Also, the rest of your outfit would suggest you're not here to catch the, uh, game," he went on, his voice growing increasingly casual.

I sat up a little taller. "What does it suggest then?" I asked.

Finally, he turned and stared at me, a playful grin on his face. "Hi, I'm Jeremiah," he said, holding out his hand.

I accepted his hand and felt it fold effortlessly into mine. "You didn't answer the question, Jeremiah," I said.

"It suggests that you'd like me to ask you out," he said, still holding lightly onto my hand.

I blinked and was unsure how to react. After a moment, I withdrew my hand from his, still feeling the warmth of his touch. "You're not from around here, are you," I said, studying his Orioles jersey.

He shook his head. "But I'm here now."

I never returned to Beanie & Co. that night. I didn't return to my apartment, either. Jeremiah had swept me clean off my feet and I barely returned to earth for seven full days. And on the eighth day? Well, that's when it all *truly* began: sporadic responses to text messages, occasionally broken plans, a high phone call frequency after 11PM.

"Well, what do you expect? He's a kid from Maryland who picked up a chick at Fenway Park. What about this is supposed to spell *true romance*, Mara?" Saul had said on day eighteen.

Saul was my ex, but we were like Jerry and Elaine from *Seinfeld* -- if Jerry had never quite gotten over Elaine, that is.

"I guess I thought there was something about this guy," I shrugged to Saul, allowing him to wrap his arms around me.

Saul sighed into my hair. "Sure, Mara," he said.

Beanie had been more supportive, using words like "romantic" and "dreamy" to describe Jeremiah.

"Even his name is sexy," she'd beamed on day forty-three.

Now, on day two-hundred seventy, I walked with my head hanging, struggling to know what to do. I heard my auntie's pearls of wisdom running through my head and thought she was probably right -- I should be alone.

Even thinking that made my heart leap into my throat, though. I had never been alone in my entire life. I always made sure to have a man on a short leash nearby at all times, ever since I was a teenager. And when I'd gotten older and finished college and moved to Somerville, I'd met Saul my first week here and we'd spent three kickass years together before I cheated on him and broke his heart. Why he took me back as a friend, I don't know, but he did, and he allowed me to let him be my crutch whenever I was *in between* relationships. Beanie said Saul did it because he hoped one day I'd wake up and realize he was *the one*.

Beanie and Saul. I once, very drunkenly, suggested that they date each other as the three of us sat around at Marvel's after the breakup with the guy before Jeremiah.

"You should fall in love," I'd said miserably. "It would serve me right. Then whenever I'd call you, you'd be together and happy and you'd get to say, 'Fuck off, Mara. Take your bullshit problems somewhere else, you miserable shit.'"

Beanie had placed her hand on my shoulder. "Let me get you a water, sweetie," she'd said.

"You'll feel better tomorrow, babe," Saul had added.

Their constant and unwavering support both electrified and depressed me. I made monumentally bad decisions about relationships all the time and neither of them ever told me I was a moron. The only person who ever did that was me -- when I took my auntie's advice and spent some time alone.

I had asked her about her famous words of wisdom once when I was in college. Why she felt that way. What prompted her dedication to it. After all, she was very happily married with four children, all of whom were just plain awesome, and, as a result, rarely alone. We were sitting beside each other on my mama's wide benched porch swing, lazily chatting about my then-boyfriend, and she'd looked away from me before she'd answer.

"Mara, the time you spend alone is the time you hear your thoughts the clearest, and there are a lot of people out there who don't want to be a part of their own inner dialogue. But there is nothing -- *nothing* -- more valuable than what you've got inside of you. Be it good or bad or enlightened or struggling, you will never get better advice than what's at your core because only you know what will make you complete. No one else can tell you. No one else can prescribe it. In moments of need, the impulse is to seek guidance and support outside of ourselves, and there is undeniable value in the love and support of others. But ultimately, you have to love and support yourself in order to accept what others have to give you." She paused and locked her eyes softly with mine. "Beautiful child, never forget that."

And I never did. But I don't think I understood it until this Tuesday night as I walked away from Jeremiah. Clearing my mind was never something I found easy, but as I moved further and further away from him, I felt the beating of my heart fill my entire body until I knew I was in command of myself, ready to listen to my gut for the first time in a very long time.

Ten minutes before I'd left Jeremiah, we'd been lying side by side on our backs in his bed feeling modestly satisfied with the evening's events. My mind felt heavy and empty all at the same time and it unnerved me.

"I'd love it if you could come with me to that work party this weekend," I'd said off the cuff.

"Would you *love it*?" he'd teased, rolling over to kiss my belly.

And there was something in that moment, something about the word *love* and his lips pressed against my vulnerable flesh that turned my mind from casual to confrontational. Flipping onto my side, I studied him with my jaw locked.

"Maybe. I dunno. Never mind," I muttered, rolling over and getting out of bed.

Jeremiah had folded his hands behind his head. "S'matter, babe?" he'd said.

I shrugged as I slid into my dress. "I'm gonna go home," I said.

Jeremiah had glanced at the clock. "It's late, Mara. You sure you wanna be out there alone?"

I paused for a moment to let the full weight of his words rest on my shoulders before drawing in a deep breath and saying, "Yes, I guess I do."

First line by Camille George

Neutral and Abnormal

"Khaki skies and a white sun -- you know what that means."

They were lying side by side on the beach staring up at a hazy dawn. She turned to him with her nose crinkled in the shape of a question mark and said, "Hmm."

His hands were propped behind his head but he drew one away to point at the ball of light in the sky. "It's happening," he said.

"What's happening?" she asked, her eyes following the stretch of his finger.

"*It*," he said smartly as he rolled over to lay half on her, his outstretched finger now brushing a strand of hair away from her eyes.

"Don't you know what this means?" he asked, incredulous.

She shook her head and waited for him to kiss her. He seemed to loom above her, his face a brighter light than that morning's sun, his eyes shining like a night's worth of stars.

But he didn't kiss her. Instead, he continued to lay half his body weight on her and said, "There's an old sailor's story about the sky -- 'Red sky at night, sailor's delight; red sky in morning, sailor's take warning.' The color of the sky over water at dawn and dusk foretells the weather."

She was starting to feel comfortable with his half-smother but she wanted him to kiss her already, so she looped her free hand around the back of his head and tilted his face towards her. "Oh?" she said.

He nodded, not taking her bait. "So this morning, the sky is neutral in color but abnormal for a morning sky." He paused and seemed to be examining her. "Your eyes are like this sky -- neutral but abnormal."

She tilted her head back a little and swallowed hard. "That's a sexy compliment," she murmured.

He rolled half off of her, causing her hand to release from the back of his neck. "Is it?" he asked, amused. "I meant it in a nice way, but *sexy*? Maybe if I'd said your eyes were unexpectedly beautiful, maybe that would sound sexy. *Neutral* and *abnormal* don't sound sexy to me."

"So how did you mean it to sound?" she asked.

He collapsed back on half of her body, his chin now resting on her chest. "I meant it to sound like the way I feel about you."

"Neutral but abnormal?" she squeaked.

He shook his head, his chin grinding into her chest. "No. I meant it to sound like I saw things in you that have yet to be invented, have yet to be labeled and stereotyped and cataloged. I meant it to sound like you're as rare as a sky that sailor's don't yet understand. I look at this sky and what it means to me is that no one knows what it means, except it's certainly a dawn of some kind. It's not exactly a warning but it's not tested, either, so anything can happen now."

At that moment, she pushed him off of her with enough force that he flopped over on his back beside her and she took that moment to pounce, starting out aggressively by pinning him into the sand and then as her face came to hover above his, she softened and let her long hair hang as a curtain around him for just an extra moment or two before she finally brought her lips to his and kissed him.

"Anything, indeed," she said, drawing back just long enough to utter the words and smile before sinking back into her attack.

First line by Shannon Robinson

A New Kind of Drug

Reality's a hell of a drug, especially when you spend the day watching people talking to thin air and sticking crayons in their ears. I'm not that brand of crazy. I'm the over-indulgent kind, the kind that thinks snorting bath salts is a good idea, the kind that believes it won't show up on a tox screen if I do it, the sort of person who doesn't even consider that maybe, just maybe, what I was snorting was laced with cocaine. Drug test, epic fail. When my doctor told me my results, she didn't even look smug or condescending about it, like she does about every other fucking thing. She actually seemed to feel a bit sorry for me. This was my version of a third strike. This was a return to rehab.

Oh, Jesus take the wheel.

I'm only nineteen years old. I don't know what the hell I'm doing. Someone says, hey, try this, it'll make you see the colors of future horizons and you'll soar towards them in a life-altering, mind-blowing way, I think to myself, why the hell not? What have I got to do on a Tuesday night besides a little time traveling?

You know, when those quacks on TV talk about things like Coors Light and pot as being the gateway to the slippery slope of hard narcotics, like X and coke, let me be the first to tell you, they are *right*. If it hadn't been for Margie Fucking Stimson's thirteenth birthday party, I would have never started drinking cheap beer and if I hadn't started with cheap beer, I wouldn't have moved up to cheap tequila by the age of thirteen-and-a-half and if I hadn't become so tight with Jose Cheapo, I would have never smoked my first joint when I was thirteen-and-a-half-and-ten-minutes-after-doing-shots-of-Jose-Cheapo. And if I hadn't smoked my first joint, I would have never agreed to try mushrooms at my fourteenth birthday party and if I had never tried mushrooms, I would have never tried acid. Dot, dot, dot... See? It's not my fault. It's Margie Fucking Stimson's Thirteenth Birthday Party's fault.

My doctor doesn't buy this theory at all. She says to me, "Jenna, if that's the case, then why the hell is Margie Fucking Stimson in drug rehabilitation therapy, too?" Insert a condescending look here. My doc, what a wise-ass. Margie Fucking Stimson's family can't afford rehab or she'd be here with me, all right. So would a bunch of those guys. We're all in the *burnout* category. I'm just the only one who's been dumb enough to get arrested. Honestly, my family can't afford to send me to rehab, either. But when it's mandated by the State, well, you fucking go.

You should see this drooler in front of me right now. What a goddamn nightmare this one is. About thirty pounds overweight, blank zombie-stare, mouth hanging open, her long ratty brown hair hasn't been washed or combed in probably forever. I think I heard the nurses calling her *Sabrina*. Sabrina, Christ, what a princess name. What a ridiculous label to stick on this vegetable. Her name should be something like Mush or Blah or Grog. Sabrina. Holy shit. Her parents got the short end of that stick. I can't help staring at her, wondering what those vacant eyes can still see. She just sits in this chair all day, almost never moving. Sometimes the nurses try to get her to do shit, like puzzles made for two-year-olds or Disney coloring books, but she barely ever responds to anything they do. Unless they try and touch her and then she nearly has a seizure. It's freaky shit when that happens. I used to like to watch it all go down, always vying for a front row seat as three nurses converge to get her pinned to the ground and stabilized, but now I just walk away when I see the situation is about to implode. I asked my doc in here if that showed a sign of growth and he just sighed. I think he thinks I'm a narcissistic waste of space. I think he might be right.

He had to deal with me on my first trip in here, about a year ago. I got busted for trying to buy heroin from an undercover cop. *Busted for heroin* does not sound good on a college application, folks, just so you know. The sad-but-true part was I wasn't even looking to buy for myself. I was curious about heroin, but I've also seen *Trainspotting* and *Requiem for a Dream*, so I was rightfully terrified of it. Most of my friends who used, even those who were pretty hardcore and had been forever, refused to shoot up, so I took that as my cue that maybe this wasn't something to fuck with. But I had just met a guy, Dario, holy shit was he a hottie, and he liked to do heroin almost exclusively. I never even saw the guy drink a beer or smoke a cigarette. The cigarette thing he and I actually had in common, so we'd started talking one day at a mutual friend's party and one thing led to another which led to me deciding it would be a nice *thank you for a nice time* to score my new friend some brown sugar.

Yeah, I never saw Dario again.

What I did see was behind-the-scenes at *One Flew Over the Cuckoo's Nest* -- and Nurse Ratchett? She lives and breaths, my friends. But in that particular stay, my doc just stared at me, the fiftieth of his two hundred patients he had to see that day, and barely said a word. I know he thought I was the dumbest person he'd ever met. I told him about Margie Fucking Stimson's birthday party and I told him about how I didn't smoke cigarettes because I was terrified of lung cancer and he just stared and stared. So I kept going. I told him about losing my virginity when I was thirteen-and-a-half-and-thirty-minutes-after-smoking-my-first-joint to a pothead named Parry, the seventeen-year-old older brother of my peer Dan who'd supplied us with both the tequila and the joints. I lost my v-card to a dude named *Parry*. Just that alone is embarrassing enough -- and then when you add on top of that that I was probably raped that night, it only gets worse. But maybe I wasn't raped. I don't know. I was thirteen. I was a blank slate of intoxication. I did that to myself. So I told my doc, you know what? I did this to myself. I fucked up, big time, and it's my fault. Well, Margie Fucking Stimson's Thriteenth Birthday Party's fault and then also my own. I did a whole mea culpa. My bad. For real. And that doctor of mine just lingered his gaze on me and then wrote some notes in his file and dismissed me. So I took the blame off of me and could sleep fine at night.

No wonder I ended up back here.

There's a sneaky bitch this time around called Anderson -- seriously, that's her name -- and she is super sappy sweet to the nurses but when the lights go out at night, we're all afraid she's gonna cut us. You should see her right now. She's sitting at a table doodling out these hilarious little cartoons she makes -- she's actually pretty talented -- but she's staring through slit eyes at this new girl Rosa. Rose just showed up two days ago but today is the first time I've seen her in the common room. Rosa's got a private room, which means she's got some money backing her up, and so we all instantly hated her. Anderson, though, she's the only one who will do something about it while those of us with our social skills still intact will be nice to her face and hate her inside. I wondered what Anderson's cartoon was about today. Just as I thought that, her calculating stare turned towards me and I smiled with a jump and immediately fix my eye on a long string of drool hanging off of Sabrina's lower lip. Someone should clean this poor bitch up. I re-focus my thought on her, wondering if Anderson was somehow able to listen into my thoughts. I wondered how Anderson was going to make Rosa feel welcomed. The last newbie was a terrified-but-determined-not-to-appear-terrified looking woman named Teresa, and she'd made the mistake of dissing one of Anderson's drawings. So Anderson told the nurses Teresa was concealing a weapon -- a pair of real scissors that Anderson had been hoarding for just such an occasion and planted in Teresa's beside drawer -- and none of us had the strength or notion to counter Anderson's story. So Teresa went to jail. Bye bye, Teresa.

This Rosa chick was gonna get it somehow.

Out of the corner of my eye, I saw Emily saunter back in the room. She's a repeat offender, like me, and our stays actually overlapped last time, too. She's cool and beautiful and so thin, it looks like a soft flick to the abdomen would break her in two. She's got a family who loves her and believes in her. I was certain she was returning from a monitored visit. No one ever came to visit me.

That's the other thing I talked to my doc on the inside and my doc on the outside about. My family couldn't be less supportive of me. No wonder I make such lousy life decisions! Couldn't I make it their fault? My mother is actually a gracious, god-fearing, church-going Methodist who cares about me but doesn't make time for me. She owns a second-hand clothing store that saps up all of her love and attention. And my father? Well, he was always around more -- he has his own architecture business and worked from home mostly -- but he wanted a son, not a daughter, so he devoted all of his love and attention to my little brother Chris. Chris, by the way, was in his junior year of high school, star of the basketball team, president of his class, and in-line to graduate in the illustrious Top Ten. Clearly, we'd made different life-choices. And while my parents had largely written me off at this point, Chris still tried to find a reason to look up to me. A week before I got sent back here, he'd posted *No one makes chocolate chip cookies like my awesome big sis* as his status update on his Facebook page. I wondered if his status update now said *No one rocks rehab like my thick headed idiot sibling*. Let's be real -- it probably should. My parents probably told him to unfriend me by now. They grew increasingly disappointed in me. But I didn't blame them.

I sat in this chair with my feet tucked up underneath me and took in the palpable sickness in the room. I was surrounded by sad stories with sad endings and sad realities. I was sobered by simply being here. I was self-conscious as I wondered what the others here thought about me, self-inflicted, over-indulgent Jenna, crashed and burned again. I basked in this overwhelming reality. I allowed it to define me. I allowed it to be my lesson-learned. I settled in. I let this be my new kind of drug. The high was unbelievable.

First line by Nate DiNardo

The Ring

"How could anyone think of hiding this under a dirty old rock?"

"Hide what, Tilly?" my mother called from the screened-in porch.

My aunt Tilly was bent in half over a some rocks at the edge of my mother's garden. I stood apprehensively nearby with the glass of water she'd requested clutched in both hands. Aunt Tilly's flower print dress billowed in the early summer breeze but she didn't move from her spot. I wondered why she didn't squat down when all of the sudden that's exactly what she did, her floral dress ballooning around her like a parachute. She seemed to be muttering to herself for a moment before one triumphant arm stuck straight up.

"This!" she declared.

I squinted my eyes to see what she had pinched between her thumb and forefinger. The sun hit it and it shone. It was a ring. I took a step closer and confirmed my first instinct -- it was a simple gold band and my aunt had unearthed it.

My mother banged through the screen door and moved swiftly towards my aunt's outstretched fingers. "What on earth..." she said.

My mother loved the phrase "What on earth." You'd think she got a commission every time she used it.

Aunt Tilly stretched back up into a standing position and rolled the ring into the palm of her hand. "Someone's broken promise," she said bitterly.

I was just a kid so I didn't know all of the in's and out's of the family drama, but I did happen to know that the reason my aunt was staying with us this summer was because Uncle Ricardo was, what on earth else, a sonovabitch, and we were likely never to see his "sorry ass face" ever again. All of this was a confessional I wasn't intended to hear because I was supposed to be in bed, but, well, I wasn't. Personally, I was glad Uncle Ricardo was gone and never to return to us -- he always smelled like sweat and said weird things to me like, "Sally, you're gonna be one hot potato someday." My name wasn't even Sally -- it was Grace -- but not according to Uncle Ricardo.

My mother had moved in so she could lean over my aunt's outstretched palm to examine the ring. "Hmm," was all she said.

Aunt Tilly's chin jutted proudly toward the sky. "Some coward hid his ring here to escape and be done with a vow he made before God and family," she declared.

"How do you know it was a man?" I asked.

Aunt Tilly's eyes snapped over towards me. "Because of the thickness of the ring, little girl. Bring me that water and don't speak again unless you are asked to speak."

My mother looked at me apologetically -- but there was no need. We all knew *how Tilly was*. It was as much a part of our family history as alcoholism and heart disease. I brought Aunt Tilly her water and stood back at what I thought would qualify as a respectful distance.

"How on earth did that end up under a rock in my garden?" my mother asked as my aunt slurped on her water.

Aunt Tilly clucked her tongue and held the ring up to examine it more carefully. "There's an inscription on the inside," she said after a moment.

My mother perked up. "Well.... What on earth does it say?"

Aunt Tilly rubbed at the dirt on the inside of the band. "Hard to say..."

"Let's go wash it in the sink!" I suggested before clapping my hand over my mouth.

My aunt glared at me for a moment before striding past. "Let's go wash it in the sink," she said.

My mother and I followed her into the house and we huddled around the sink as Aunt Tilly ran the ring under the water faucet for a few moments before holding it up in the light once more.

"*'Por los siglos,'*" she read slowly. And after a moment she closed her eyes and added, "*de los siglos.*"

"What on earth does it mean, Tilly?" my mother asked.

My aunt spun around and sank dramatically into a kitchen chair. "It means 'until the end of time.' It means 'forever and ever.' It means 'eternity.'" She bowed her head for a moment before looking back at my mother. "This ring is inscribed 'Por los siglos' -- and I would be willing to bet that his bride's ring is inscribed with the balance of the phrase - 'de los siglos.'" She let the ring clatter down onto the table and pressed flat palms against her forehead. "Fuck," she said.

"Tilly," my mother admonished.

Aunt Tilly shrugged. "Grace is going to learn the word anyway -- she might as well learn it in a justifiable context."

My mother shot me a sharp look. "Don't say that word," she said.

"Yes, ma'am," I said, happy that I wasn't being dismissed from the room.

"All this ring is," my aunt went on, "is proof that love isn't forever. It doesn't matter what vows you exchange or what you inscribe on gold that is blessed by a priest. This phrase means nothing without the other half -- it's just bad grammar right now. It means nothing once it's off the finger and buried under a rock in some anonymous backyard. Abandoned forever by some coward who was too afraid to hand it to the woman who he promised to love *forever*."

"Maybe he just lost it," I suggested. "Maybe he's been looking for it. Maybe we could find him and give it back!"

Aunt Tilly's hand flew out and struck me across the face.

"Tilly!" my mother yelled, hauling me towards her. I was stunned. No one had ever hit me before. As my mother hugged me close and gingerly touched the spot where a light red impression of my aunt's hand surfaced. We both looked across the table at my aunt whose face was growing darker by the moment.

"You can't give anyone *forever* back, Grace," my aunt said slowly. "Forever is gone. Forever is a fairy tale. Forever was buried under a rock in your back yard."

My mother and I watched Aunt Tilly grab the ring before she got up from the table and to bang through the back door. What she did with the ring, we never found out -- we just never saw it again.

First line by Bob Hunsche

Punchline

Sometimes I miss the punchline.

Like, the other day, I walked into the room and everyone was already laughing. I was too late. No one told me what was so funny. I didn't ask, either. I figured if it was relevant, someone would have just told me the joke. Since no one did, I just moved in and out of the room like a ghost, no one even noticed. If I really was a ghost, I wonder if I'd be able to read people's minds, I wonder if I'd be able to see behind their eyes and witness the laughter first hand. I wonder if I'd think it was funny.

Sometimes I think I miss the punchlines even when they play out in front of me.

I don't get invited to very many parties anymore. I used to, when I was younger, especially when I was a child. I think mothers would just look at their child's class list and hand write an invitation for everyone on the roster, whether their child liked all of those people or not. I think that's how I kept getting invited. I would come to the party and I would sit quietly at the picnic table and lightly grasp a cookie in both of my hands and nibble on it while the other kids raced around, making up nicknames and tackling each other to the ground. The hosting mother would always come to me and say, "Why don't you go and play?" and I would withdraw one hand from the cookie and point and say, "I can't grass stain my clothes or my mother will be upset." The hosting mother would stare oddly at me and walk away, even though I'd said a perfectly reasonable thing.

I didn't get asked to attend as many parties once I was more of an adolescent. I guess it's more difficult for mothers to fill out invitations using a yearbook as a guide instead of a solitary class roster. I assume I didn't get invited because most of my peers found me extremely odd and maybe even a little off-putting. I was tested for Asperger's Syndrome when I was in the fourth grade and the test came back conclusive, though it took my mother a long time to tell me -- years even. I was in the tenth grade when I finally overheard her telling my aunt, who is my father's sister and her best friend -- and I cocked my head and said, "Well, I always wondered about that," and wasn't upset. I think that made my mother and my aunt even more upset that I wasn't upset. Who becomes upset when someone's not upset? I don't understand.

That's one of the side effects -- I don't understand a lot of things. *Especially* punchlines. So no one tells me jokes. It's not that they never did. New people always try. New people are an oddity to me. They smile so hugely and speak slowly and loudly as if I'm hearing impaired. So I mime them -- because maybe they are hearing impaired.

They are never hearing impaired.

I'm off-putting to them, too, once they are no longer new.

My father understands me the best. He memorized all of the state flowers with me and followed my obsession with plants and always tried to stay one step ahead of what my interests were in the field of botany -- he taught me the word botany, also -- and he got me a job volunteering at a greenhouse at a university where he worked as a biology professor and when I was old enough, they gave me a job, and I work there still. My father did that for me. I try to tell new people about my father and they listen politely and make an excuse to back away. I wonder if they would ignore me if I was a ghost haunting this greenhouse.

I wonder what it's like to be someone people like.

I asked my father once why he liked me, since no one else really did. He said, "People like you -- they just don't know anyone else who loves plants as much as you do, so they don't know what to say." I think he was lying to me, but I didn't say so. Maybe he was right. I do love plants more than most people. I think he was just being kind. I don't understand kindness usually, but what my father said made me feel warm, so I think it's a good thing.

Before he died, I came and sat beside him in his hospital bed because my mother said that my chances to do so where running out. When he saw me, he smiled. He could probably smell the greenhouse on me. After a moment, he looked up at me and said very slowly, "An arborist can count to Tree."

My eyes flew open wide. I got it. And I laughed.

First line by Lee Wesolowski

The Circus Donkey

Once upon a time a circus donkey sat on a full whoopee cushion, but the cushion failed to make a sound. The make-up-less clown stood stunned beside his assigned animal with his arms frozen out in a gesture of *ta-da!* as someone on the sidelines yelled, "Cut, cut, cut!" The rehearsal came to a standstill and everyone stared at the donkey, sitting as he'd been trained to do, his eyes darting wildly at all the attention rushing towards him.

"Get up," the donkey's trainer muttered, flashing a hand sign that the animal understood more readily than sarcasm and wit. "It's deflated," the trainer reported, waving the whoopee cushion in the air.

"Well, what the fuck," the show's director said. "Fill it up and try it out."

So the trainer inflated the cushion and the make-up-less clown rolled his eyes and said, "I'm getting a cigarette in," as a group clustered in close to the trainer to see what would happen on Take #2. The trainer pressed the cushion between his palms and it let out a sound to rival flatulence and all of the adults nodded confidently that the prop was working.

"Let's try it with the donkey this time," the director said.

So the trainer set it up and signed to the donkey what he was supposed to do and when he sat down on the whoopee cushion, they could have heard a pin drop -- silence once more.

"Seriously, what's the deal?" the director barked.

The trainer signed for the donkey to stand once more and the clown had returned from his cigarette break right then and no one really seemed to know what to do, so the clown sat down on the cushion.

Pffftttbbblllmmmmttt!

"See, it works just fine," the clown said from the ground.

"Why didn't it do that when the donkey sat down?" the director asked, his eyes boring holes first into the clown on the floor and then into the trainer and then into the donkey who merely swished his tail while the humans lifted their shoulders into shrugs.

"I'll set it up again," the trainer said.

"This is costing us money!" the director hollered. "We need to get this gag right. The show's music will skip a beat when that donkey sits on that whoopee cushion. If it doesn't work, it'll be catastrophic."

The clown chuckled. "Unlivable," he added. "We'll have to do a mass suicide if the donkey doesn't do his job correctly."

"It's an important gag," the director growled. "Let's try it again -- with the music this time."

Everyone stood back as the clown and the donkey took their spots in the center ring along with the other showmen who'd been sitting idly by since this prop malfunction issue began. When the director waved his hand, a brassy band blared over the loudspeaker as the showmen dove into their routine and everyone held a collective breath when it came time for that donkey to sit down once more.

Silence.

"I'm gonna murder that fucking donkey!" the director chortled.

The trainer and clown both dove in front of the animal to blockade the director's forward charge.

"He can't help it -- he's just an ass!" the clown yelled.

The director stopped his charge mid-stride and doubled over laughing, thus giving the cast and crew permission to cackle along with him and the donkey, without any signal from the trainer, stood up and bent his front legs into a sweeping bow, as if he understood there was a gag and he'd just played a starring role.

And that, boys and girls, is how a well-timed pun stopped a crazed circus director from ripping a donkey limb from limb in front of an entire room full of people and the donkey went on to live many happy years at a petting zoo where his show biz past allowed him the honor of playing the role of "Donkey" in the nativity play of many local churches at Christmas time and play it he would to great acclaim, likely because he did not have to sit on any whoopee cushions since they were not present at the birth of Jesus Christ.

First line by Bill Anderson

Rabbit Rabbit

What if everything I thought was true wasn't? I sucked in a deep breath when I saw my parents making their way into the baggage claim area and half-wished a voice would come on the loudspeaker declaring, "Cara McCleod, you're actually adopted and your real parents are waiting for you by Baggage Carousel 4." But that didn't happen and the dopey smiling faces of Robert and Catherine McCleod maintained their rapid approach to where I'd found a phone booth to lean against. Phone booths, what archaic nothings! I felt ironic slumped against one waiting for the only two people left in the known universe with not only a land-line but phones that still had cords on them. A visit to my childhood home was my own personal hell.

"Cara, I love your new pink hair!" my mother declared, her hands thrown wide to embrace me.

"Um, thanks, Mom," I said warily, unsure of whether or not she actually liked my shock-effect-for-the-parental-visit dye job.

"I'm sure it's not a cry for help," my father said sarcastically, and I felt smugly justified. At least one of the 'rents found me obnoxious and beyond parenting.

"Oh, Robert, stop it," my mother said, pulling back from me and swatting playfully at him. "Cara's always been artistic."

"She can be artistic with the brown hair god gave her," my father harrumphed.

"This isn't Palmer, Iowa," my mother continued. "This is Boston, Massachusetts. I'm sure Cara's just trying to stand out."

"She could stand out by opening her mouth and saying useful things," my father harumphed, still staring disdainfully at my freshly pink hair.

"And she can't open her mouth and say useful things with her pink hair?" my mother inquired.

"Probably no one would listen to her," my father said.

"Well, I would," my mother staunchly defended.

"You're her mother. You have to. But important people, people who offer employment, they would not."

"Gwen Stefani has pink hair," my mother said, still desperate to win this argument.

My mother was weirdly obsessed with Gwen Stefani. I didn't get that, either.

"Who?" my father asked, clearly thrown off track.

"She's a rock star, Robert, and people listen to her," my mother said.

I think even she knew playing the Gwen Stefani card was going to get her an "L" in the Robert and Catherine McCleod Win/Loss Official Argument Score Card.

"MTV ruined this country!" my father yelled.

"OK, just settle down," I finally interrupted. "It's temporary dye, Dad, it's not a big deal."

"Oh," he said, regaining his composure.

"Say hello to your daughter, Robert," my mother urged.

My father leaned in and gave me a stiff hug. "Hello, Cara. The pink hair is an abomination."

"Thanks, Dad," I said cheerily.

It was going to be a long weekend. But first we had to gather their luggage.

"How was the flight?" I asked as we positioned ourselves by their designated Carousel 3.

"Fine," they said in unison. Unbelievable. They were already back on the same page. Pink hair abominations and MTV be damned -- they cannot destroy the union of these two beautiful Midwestern souls.

"Any good stewardess stories, Dad?" I asked, jabbing him in the ribs with my elbow. My father had a weird obsession with stewardesses that almost matched my mother's Gwen Stefani abnormality.

My father snorted. "We got the gay," he said a little too loudly.

"The what?" I repeated sweetly.

"The gay. The gay guy. His name was Geoffrey-with-a-G -- he told us. More like Geoffrey-with-a-gay." My father truly thought he was witty.

"He was fine," my mother said, patting my arm as if it was concerning me that *the gay* did not properly service my father.

"He told your mother she had a pretty smile," my father went on. "As if he knew."

"You don't think a homosexual can tell if someone has a pretty smile?" I asked, for research purposes.

"Well, not on a woman," my father said indignantly.

I choked back a laugh. "Oh, right," I said. "Because he can only appreciate such beauty in a fellow man."

My father shifted uncomfortably. "All I know is there were two other perfectly lovely female stewardesses and we got the gay."

"Well, look on the bright side," I said cheerily. "They were probably lesbians. It was probably an all-gay flight crew."

My mother laughed a little too quickly, followed by, "How's school, Cara?"

I was a junior at the New England School of Art and Design studying Illustration. Shrugging, I said, "Fine."

"Are you still getting all A's?" she pushed.

I shrugged again. "Won't know until the end of the term," I said.

"Well, what are you working on right now?" she asked.

"An original," I said. "It's called *Rabbit, Rabbit.*"

"Oh?" my mother said.

"Yup," I said, grateful that the luggage was finally starting to appear on the conveyor belt.

"Well, tell your parents about it," my mother insisted.

With my eyes glued to the luggage as it passed, I said, "It's about a superstitious rabbit."

"Huh?" my father said.

"It's a thing. On the first of every month, you're supposed to say 'Rabbit, rabbit' for good luck."

"Why?" my father asked.

"I don't know, Dad, it's just a thing. A superstition."

"What, are you into witchcraft now?" my father asked, once again a little too loudly.

I weighed my answer options and finally decided on, "No, Dad." Just the easier path. "Anyway, the story's about a rabbit who forgets to say 'Rabbit, rabbit' on the first of the month and has all these bad luck things happen to him."

"That sounds nice," my mother said encouragingly.

"Yeah, then at the end, he realizes if he just thought before he acted, he wouldn't keep falling into neighbor's rabbit holes uninvited or eating the rotten carrots, that sorta thing. Like, think before you act. Like, we make our own luck. Like, don't be an idiot who makes bad decisions and then blame them on something as arbitrary as *luck*," I continued.

My father's eyes drifted back to my pink hair and grunted.

Just then, I saw my mother's bright red paisley Vera Bradley luggage come out on the conveyor belt with my father's navy blue bag with the large yellow and white striped bow, my mother's addition, follow suit.

"Goody," my mother said with a delighted clap.

I couldn't help but smile. They were total disasters, but they were my disasters. As we gathered their bags and headed out to grab a taxi back to my North End apartment, I said, "Wait til I show you guys my new tattoo!"

I was pleasantly rewarded by my father's bellowed response:

"IT BETTER NOT BE ONE OF THOSE SLUT STAMPS!"

"Tramp Stamp, Dad, it's called a Tramp Stamp," I said, gently patting his arm.

"I think Gwen Stefani has one of those," my mother said supportively.

Oh, yes, it was true -- I was a lucky girl.

First line by Lee Wesolowski

These Boots Were Made for Walkin'

I got all the way to Park Street before I realized I was wearing mismatching boots. I was a total shame factory. I looked around me, sure that I'd find a dozen pairs of eyes judging me harshly but no one seemed to notice. Hell, I hadn't even noticed and I'd been wearing these boots for nearly an hour. I stared at my feet intensely for a full minute, trying to decide if it was an innocent enough mistake or not. The boots were similar in that they were both black and flat and required a zip-up. But otherwise, they were pretty different -- one had a fake buckle on the side, the other had a silver embellishment. How had I managed this fashion travesty? I sighed and got off the train.

Above ground on the Boston Common, even fewer people would take notice of me, but I still felt self-conscious. Even so, I looked around at the packs of Emerson College undergrads, all "artistically" dressed in "ironic" clothes and the business professionals and the ever-present clusters of homeless people and took note of every pair of shoes I saw walk by me. Even the homeless people were matching -- even the Emerson students. But not me. I had officially *gone 'round the bend*, a favorite expression of my mother's.

I was now quoting my mother!

There was no end to this.

I walked the three blocks to the temp agency where I worked as a mid-level manager (a vague enough job title to seem acceptable without garnering many further questions). Ordinarily, I strolled in the office casually, stopping to say hi to my friends who have yet to be promoted out of this pool of worker bees before ascending the staircase to my own bland cubicle -- but it was my *own* -- and checking my standard seventy-five waiting emails. But today, I scurried by the long tables where the drones sat staring at computer screens, bumping elbows with their co-workers. I would not be judged by them.

When I got to my cube, I immediately took off my boots and slipped my feet into a pair of clogs I kept under my desk. The relief was instantaneous.

"Morning, Marla," a voice said behind me.

"Morning, Krista," I replied as I turned around.

Krista was also a mid-level manager at this temp agency. We'd been promoted at the same time, even though I'd worked here six weeks longer than her. But we'd overcome that difference between us easily when our cubes were set up next to each other and we realized that we'd traded up to our own space (no more elbow-to-elbow with some guy named Bob!), but this world was just an elevated version of what we'd been doing. Translation: we were simultaneously bored out of our minds and overtaxed, unchallenged and mindless yet intensely focused and pressured. We'd both gone to school for artistic pursuits -- she had a MFA in illustration and I had a bachelors in writing -- and we both worked here. You can imagine the flatness of our souls at this point.

"I wore mismatching shoes," I told her, pointing at my boots under the desk.

Krista mused for a moment and then asked, "Want some coffee?"

I'd been at my desk for a full thirty seconds. "Sure, I could use a break," I said. Krista and I walked down the florescently lit hallway to the manager's break room, easily one of our favorite places because the whole wall was windows looking out over the city. There's just something about being able to see outside that most people probably take for granted. People like Krista and me, we almost never get to look out the window, so we spend as much time here as productivity will allow. We poured our coffee and sat at one of the tables for a full five minutes without talking.

"Well, I gotta take the rest of this back to my desk," Krista said.

I nodded and we returned to our neighboring cubes.

I opened my inbox and tried not to feel immediately tired. Instead, my mind started to wander to the mismatching boots beneath my desk. How *had* that happened? I thought back to an hour ago, scurrying around my Cambridge apartment, trying to avoid my obnoxious roommate and feed my cat. I just wasn't paying attention, I decided, and that bummed me out. I prided myself on being organized and together. Clearly, this boot issue was the first step in my road to complete and total chaos. I was doomed.

I worked steadily through the morning and into the early part of the afternoon. Around one, I slid back in my rolling chair and asked Krista if she was ready for lunch. She stuck a finger in the air to indicate "one minute" and continued to speak smoothly to some client, probably, on the phone. While she wrapped things up, I stood and stretched.

"You guys headed to lunch?" asked another mid-leveler named Hugh.

I nodded, flashing him the same finger Krista'd flashed me.

"OK, wait for me. You're going out, right?" Hugh asked.

I nodded vaguely. We usually did. I tugged at my skirt as Hugh walked away -- all this eating out had shrunken my clothes, it seemed. But there was an Au Bon Pain in the lobby of our building and their mac-n-cheese was incredible, so who could blame me? Don't I deserve a bright happy spot in my otherwise mind-numbing day? Day after day, I decided I did. As I waited for Krista to get off the phone and Hugh to return, I did a few side stretches. That counted as exercise, right?

Fifteen minutes later, I was spooning that rich and creamy mac-n-cheese in my mouth as if it was to be my last meal on earth. Krista and I used to come here and get salads with dressing on the side. Now she was unapologetically eating an Italian sub. Hugh was eating a fruit cup -- with a side of two reubens. What was wrong with us?

As we walked back to the office, my eye inadvertently went to the feet of every person walking by. All of them seemed to be sporting matching shoes. My inadequacy set back in, despite the fact that my clogs qualified as matching shoes. Back at my desk, I managed to half-focus on my work for the rest of the afternoon, but the closer it came to being time to call it quits, the more stressed out I became. I was going to have to put my mismatched boots on.

And once they were on, I was going to have to go and meet up with my boyfriend so I could dump him, just as I'd been planning ever since we set up this date two days ago. Dumping him was one thing -- dumping him while in an idiotic wardrobe oversight was a whole other helpline.

"You could just wear your clogs," Krista said with a shrug ten minutes before we were to leave. "But really, David's not going to notice you're wearing two different boots."

"Yes, but *I* will know," I moaned. "And these clogs aren't great for walking around the city -- soles are too thin."

Krista's expression didn't change. "Just wear the boots and move on," she said simply.

Easy for her to say.

I debated it for a few more minutes before taking Krista's advice. No matter what was on my feet, David needed to get his walking papers tonight. I couldn't postpone due to footwear.

We were to meet at the Beantown Pub, the midway point between our two offices, around six o'clock. The bar was relatively empty despite the after work crowd potential. I arrived a few minutes before him and sat at a table by the window and ordered two Maker's on the rocks. The waitress was just setting the drinks down when he arrived, his round, friendly face beaming first at me and then at the drink.

"How's your day?" he asked, kissing me on the cheek before sitting down.

"Usual," I said lightly.

David then launched into a story about his co-workers Devon and Larissa, one more gorgeous than the next, and their hilarious good time working on a presentation for a conference in Florida next week. I smiled tightly and nodded politely, forcing a laugh when it seemed necessary. I wondered if he could tell I was tensing up for the breakup. I searched his eyes to see what I could find.

We'd been dating off and on for the last four years, though we'd been mostly "on" for the last year and a half. Part of me loved him with soul-dropping force. But part of me -- part of me wanted to run away every time he locked his eyes with mine. He was too "made" for me -- too much my checklist of the perfect guy -- and with such perfection comes the ultimate flaw: perfection. Don't act so surprised -- I am a woman -- these are my inner-ramblings.

When he finished his story, I reached over and placed a hand on his. As soon as I did so, his eyes widened. It was as if my touch was a preview of coming attractions. I didn't look away or avoid his direct gaze. Instead, I inhaled deeply and said, "I think it's time we saw other people."

David froze for a moment and then got a bit red in the face. "Why?" he asked. "Things have been so great between us. We've talked about you moving in with me. Marla."

The way he said my name -- God, it hit me in the gut. "I know," I said weakly. "I'm sorry. I can't move in with you. I can't be with you anymore."

"Why?" he asked again.

The whole speech I had prepared about how we'd grown apart and wanted different things slipped out of my mind and I stared at the ground. "I just..." There was a long pause where my gaze remained focused on the floor -- and then I caught sight of my mismatched boots. Looking back up at him, I said, "I'm a mess, David."

"What?" he asked.

"I'm not even wearing matching shoes today. That's how out of it I am. I never used to be this way. I never used to be so flaky and dispassionate. I used to have a never ending stream of stories to tell you at the end of my day, but now I can't think of one thing to tell you besides 'my shoes don't match.' I just need some time... Some time to become *me* again."

"And you think the only way you can do that is alone?" he asked.

I nodded slowly. "I am unhappy, David. And it's not your fault, but you're not how I'm going to lift myself out of this, either. You're in a good place right now and I want you to stay there. I need to get to a good place, but I don't know that our good places are going to align the same way. So it's not that I think I have to do this alone -- I just think I have to do it without you."

"You should quit your job," David said. "*That's* the problem. *I'm* not the problem."

I pulled a twenty dollar bill out of my wallet and put it on the table. "No," I said. "*I* am the problem."

Walking out of the bar, I felt an air of neutrality hit me and it never even occurred to me to cry as I headed back to Park Street station so I could go home and walk around barefoot for awhile.

First line by Sarah Bayle

Hilarious

"A gorilla walks into a bar and orders a banana martini. 'A talking gorilla. That's odd,' thinks the bartender. 'I must be dreaming.' He tries to wake himself up. His eyes open, he's in bed in his room. He was dreaming. He carefully eyes his wife laying next to him for a small moment. Then he turns away from her and lets a silent tear fall because his marriage is in shambles."

Shelly stared at Bert with her mouth hanging open as they sat side by side on a bench in Davis Square. "What?" she said.

He grinned wide, ear-to-ear, and said, "Isn't that *hilarious*?"

Shelly closed her mouth and then opened it again to speak. "*What?*" she repeated.

Bert exhales deeply and rolls his eyes. "It's a joke, Shelly! You're supposed to laugh."

"The punchline to the gorilla ordering a banana martini is the bartender's marriage is in shambles?" she squeaked.

"Yes! You *do* get it," Bert said, clapping a hand on her shoulder.

"No, no I *don't* get it," Shelly said. "It's not funny."

"Would it be funnier or less funny if I told you it was a true story and the bartender then got the idea to be a gorilla for Halloween?" Bert asked, staring disappointingly at her.

"That's not a punchline!" Shelly shrilled. "None of those are punchlines!"

"*But that's why it's funny*," Bert said. "I thought you had a quirky sense of humor."

"Yeah, but in the way that I find *Portlandia* or Christopher Guest movies to be funny, not non-jokes. Then *anything* is a joke. *Everything* is a joke. They can't *all* be jokes!" Shelly huffed.

"Well, why not? Maybe that's some poor guy's life, right? Maybe he thought there was going to be a hilarious payoff to his gorilla dream and instead, all he got was his crappy real life with a wife that's probably cheating on him with his secretary or something and, you know what, that shit is funny!" Bert insisted.

"How is that funny?" Shelly asked.

"Have you ever seen the movie *Melinda and Melinda*?" Bert asked.

"The Woody Allen flick?" Shelly asked.

"That's the one," Bert said.

"He's a pervert so I skipped it on principle," Shelly sniffed.

It was Bert's turn to pause and gape his mouth. "Seriously? That is completely bonkers, but OK. Anyway, the premise of *Melinda and Melinda* is there is a fine line between comedy and tragedy. The movie starts out with a group of writers in a cafe discussing this topic and then they're given a premise -- a dinner party in Manhattan when an unexpected guest arrives -- and from there, the movie splits in two, one with a comedic take on this scenario and one with a tragic take. It's really a brilliant film. You should get off your high horse and see it," Bert said.

"But the joke -- the story -- you told is just tragic," Shelly said weakly. "A broken marriage, a single tear -- those are all terrible, unfunny things."

Bert shrugged. "It's a *silent* tear, not a *single* tear, but anyway, it all depends on how you look at it. The way I look at it, I was expecting a hilarious payoff and because the end of the joke is so unexpected, it struck me as especially funny. When I heard it, I laughed until I cried -- but the happy kind of crying. It's like a joke with Asperger's -- no social grace at all."

"My nephew has Asperger's," Shelly flinched. "It's horrible."

Bert sighed. "You are missing the point," he said.

"Which is?" Shelly quipped.

"The point is absurdity is funny! The joke's meant to make you feel a bit uncomfortable and that, too, is funny. I really think you should stop telling people you have a quirky sense of humor," Bert said, matter-of-factly.

Shelly pursed her lips and looked away. "You're rude," she said.

"You're uptight," he said.

Shelly jumped to her feet. "I'm gonna go now," she said. And then she turned to glare at him. "For the record, this is the most pointless blind date I've ever been on."

"Oh yeah?" Bert said, eyebrows raised. "You should probably go delete your OK Cupid account as soon as you get home because the internet is full of worse dates than this one, I can promise you."

"*Worse* I can handle," Shelly spat. "It's the *pointless* that's the killer."

Bert watched her stalk away and chuckled into a final sigh. "That's hilarious," he mused. "I'm gonna marry that girl."

The opening bit was originally told to me/supplied by the king of the anti-joke Tom Lada.

The Policy Violation

"I am legally obligated to tell you this conversation is being recorded."

Paul's head dropped towards his chest. "Yeah, OK, Jack," he said.

"OK," his boss said, clearing his throat. "I need to ask you about last Friday night."

"Yeah," Paul said, not looking up.

"You were working," his boss said.

"Yeah," Paul said.

"Alone," his boss added.

"Yeah," Paul said.

"Tell me, did anything unusual happen that night?" his boss asked.

"Yeah, Jack," Paul said, looking up.

"Could you tell me what happened?" his boss prompted.

"Mrs. Gomez brought her dog in the store and her dog took a shit over by the dairy case," Paul said.

"What kind of dog does Mrs. Gomez have?" his boss asked.

"Little one. A poodle or a shih tzu or something. It's white," Paul said.

"Is Mrs. Gomez allowed to bring her dog in the store?" his boss asked.

Paul shifted. "Nah, she ain't supposed to. But she does it all the time."

"Did you ask her to curb her dog?" his boss asked.

Paul shifted again. "Nah, I mean, I know she ain't supposed to, but..."

"I know, she does it all the time. Despite the fact that we have asked her not to," his boss said.

"Right," Paul said.

"So Mrs. Gomez brings her dog illegally into the store..."

"Technically, it's just against policy," a silent-until-now man in a suit interjected.

"Who are you?" Paul asked, as if this person had suddenly materialized before his eyes.

"Lawyer," the man said, seemingly evaporating into the mist once his legalize was recognized.

Paul's boss rolled his eyes and set out to rephrase. "So Mrs. Gomez brings her dog into the store, even though it's against policy and despite you asking her verbally not to bring her dog into the store..."

"Actually, Jack, I didn't ask her not to bring the dog in," Paul said.

His boss looked dumbfounded. "Why the fuck not? You know the rules around here."

Paul shrugged. "She does it all the time. You know she'll ignore me if I ask her to curb her dog. And she wasn't my only customer. Oh, and I didn't realize she had even come in until someone came and told me the dog shit on the floor."

His boss leaned back and folded his arms across his chest. "Well, which is it, Paul? Did you just ignore her coming in the store with the dog in direct violation to store policy or did you not see her right away because you were with a customer?"

"Customer, I was with a customer," Paul said, a slow, wide smile taking over his face. "I didn't see her come in. Smelled the shit, though!"

His boss sighed and rubbed his hand against his face. "OK, so you didn't see her come in, but she did come in with the dog, even though it's against the rules for her to do so. And then her dog shit on the floor in front of the dairy case."

"Yes, that's what happened Jack."

OK," his boss said, tapping the table near the tape recorder. "How did you discover the dog had shit on the floor?"

"Well, it's not a huge store, so it was pretty easy to figure out," Paul said.

"But how, specifically, did you find out?" his boss asked.

"A customer came over and told me," Paul said. "An old Asian lady I'd never seen before. She came up to the counter and said, 'That dog shit over there' but with a funny Asian accent that I can't do."

His boss rolled his eyes. "What did you do?"

"I said, 'That's gross, man,' and the Asian lady left."

"Was she going to buy stuff?" his boss asked.

"Probably. You don't usually come into a convenience store to check out the cool displays or see if there's any new running shoes in stock or whatever," Paul said.

"So we lost her sale," his boss said.

"Well, she didn't buy anything, so I guess so," Paul said.

"Why do you think she didn't buy what she likely came in to buy?" his boss asked.

"Because Mrs. Gomez' dog shit on the floor," Paul said.

"OK," his boss said, brightening up. "What happened next?"

"Well, I went over to see if the Asian lady was right."

"Was she?"

Paul gulped and nodded slowly. "Oh, she was right, alright."

"Tell us what you witnessed," his boss said.

"I witnessed Mrs. Gomez reaching into the dairy case for a half gallon of 2% as her dog sniffed its fresh shit on the floor," Paul said.

"Did Mrs. Gomez seem to notice the... mess her dog had created?" his boss asked.

"Nah, I don't think so," Paul said. "She's real fond of yelling things like 'Clean up in aisle fourteen,' which is just annoying because we don't even have fourteen aisles..."

"Paul, focus," his boss said.

"Oh, right, sorry, Jack," Paul said.

"What happened next?" his boss asked.

"So Mrs. Gomez has her milk and she starts walking towards me, yanking the dog behind her..."

"Yanking?" his boss interrupted. He turned to the lawyer. "Can we sue for animal abuse as well?" he asked.

"No," the lawyer said before evaporating once more.

"OK, fine," his boss said. "So she's walking away from the scene of the crime..."

"Policy violation," the lawyer interrupted.

"Right, OK, policy violation," his boss echoed. "What then?"

"So I stopped her and said, 'Hey, Mrs. Gomez, your dog had an accident,' and she said, 'What, an accident? In the store?? I'll sue you!' and then she laughed really loudly and kind of close to my ear," Paul said.

"She threatened legal action against you?" his boss fumed.

"I think she was mostly kidding," Paul said, shifting again. "But it *is* what she said, so I don't know."

His boss closed his eyes and took a moment to breath deeply. Re-opening them, he said in a calm voice, "Please continue."

"Sure, OK. So I said, 'No, Mrs. Gomez, your dog... pooped on the floor.'" Paul paused to grimace. "I hate the word 'poop,'" he said.

His boss rolled his eyes. "Go on..."

"Right, so I pointed to the mess her dog made and Mrs. Gomez got a little red in the face said, 'So?' So I asked her to clean it up because it was her dog's mess and she knew she wasn't supposed to have the dog in the store anyway and she got even redder in the face and said, 'Why don't you just get the mop and clean it up like it was a rat turd since you've probably got a rat infestation problem and have to clean shit up all the time anyway' -- except she said poop, I think -- and I said, 'No, Mrs. Gomez, we don't have a rat problem and it's not my job to clean up after your dog,' and she said, 'It's a mess on your floor, so it *is* your job' and I said, 'But you're not even supposed to have your dog in here and you know that' and she said, 'You already said that, Paul,' and I said, 'Well, it's not less true now than when I said it the first time,' and she said, 'Well, I'm not cleaning it up,' and she handed me five dollars for the milk and stormed out of the store."

All three men were silent for a moment.

"What did you do then?' his boss asked quietly.

"I called you," Paul said with a *duh* edge to his voice.

"And what did I do?" his boss asked.

"You told me to have a professional cleaning service come in and we'd bill Mrs. Gomez," Paul said.

"So did you do that?" his boss asked.

"Yeah," Paul said.

"And how quickly did the cleaning service get there?" his boss asked.

"Like twenty minutes later," Paul said. "That's a bio hazard issue."

"And were we charged an extra fee for that rushed service?" his boss asked.

"Yeah," Paul said with a hefty laugh. "It was crazy expensive. Like a hundred dollars. To clean up dog shit."

His boss shifted his jaw. "But it was professionally cleaned."

"Cleanest that spot on the floor has ever been," Paul affirmed. "My girlfriend's an awesome cleaning lady."

"You called your girlfriend?" the lawyer interjected.

"She has a cleaning service," Paul said with a shrug. "Who else is going to come right over at eleven p.m. on a Friday?"

The lawyer turned to his boss. "You didn't mention the cleaning service was owned by his girlfriend."

"What's the difference?" his boss asked.

It was the lawyer's turn to shift uncomfortably. "It could be a problem," he said stiffly, evaporating once more.

His boss rolled his eyes. "So we got this bill for $100 to have Mrs. Gomez' dog's shit cleaned up off the floor. What happened next, Paul?"

"We waited until she came back in the store and handed her the bill," Paul said.

"When was she back?" his boss asked.

"I mean, the next day. She's not the brightest bulb," Paul said, tapping his skull.

"Did she have the dog with her?" his boss asked.

Paul laughed. "Yes! That's the best part!"

"What happened?"

I asked her to curb her dog and handed her the cleaning bill and she got all red-faced again and said she wasn't going to pay *or* curb her dog," Paul said.

"And then?" his boss said.

"And then she stormed out of the store," Paul said.

"Did she take the bill with her?" his boss asked.

"Nah," Paul said.

"So then what happened?" his boss asked.

"I called you and you cursed a lot and then you said you were getting a lawyer and then a few days after that, you asked me if I could come in for this interview. On the record," Paul said, tapping the table near the tape recorder.

"Yes," his boss said. He turned to the lawyer. "What else do we need?" he asked. The lawyer sat motionless.

"OK, I guess that's it, Paul. Thanks," his boss said, turning the tape recorder off.

"This one's going all the way to the Supreme Court, Jack," Paul said, extended his hand.

His boss shook it. "Policy violators across the globe will learn a very valuable lesson."

"I hope so," Paul said. "Because if Mrs. Gomez doesn't cough up the cash for that bill, my girlfriend's cleaning service is going to sue us for neglecting to pay her fee, so... Chop chop."

His boss said nothing with his arms folded across his chest.

First line by Leslie Drescher

Vodkamelon

"I can't believe I ate the whole thing."

Dave turned his head to see his girlfriend Amy bent perfectly in half over the kitchen counter. Shaking his head in a simultaneous chuckle, he turned back to the Red Sox game. "Babe, we're barely out of the first inning," he said.

Amy groaned and lolled her head to the side. "Anyone else coming over?"

He shrugged and checked his phone. "Maybe Phil and Kara. And maybe Ellis, Ron, and Steve."

"So it's bad that I just ate all of that," she mumbled.

Dave turned up the volume on the TV. "Bad that you ate an entire container of vodka soaked watermelon? I guess that depends on your definition of 'bad.'"

"Your friends already hate me. Now they're gonna think I'm a boozebag."

"Babe, you *are* a boozebag."

Amy's body jerked off the counter and she stood almost upright. "You're really not supposed to agree with me when I say derogatory things about myself, *babe*."

Dave exhaled deeply and stood up to move towards her. "I thought this was a 'same page' situation, Ames, I'm sorry." He kissed her lightly on the nose and she fell into his warm grasp.

"Same-page me over to the couch with you, please," she said.

"Sure thing, Boozy McGee," Dave said cheerfully.

She smacked him lightly with the back of her hand. "Dick."

"We can play with it later, babe, right now we're expecting company," Dave said, plopping her on the couch.

"It's not fair. You're too sober," Amy moaned.

"Well, what were you thinking, eating all of that vodkamelon?" Dave asked.

Amy shrugged. "Didn't realize you'd soaked them. Thought it was just watermelon. For like half the container."

Dave chuckled. "Seriously, babe? You're innocent as a fawn on the first day of spring."

"Retort!" Amy declared, jabbing her finger in the air.

"What's that now?"

"I couldn't think of a comeback so I just yelled 'Retort!' as a substitute," Amy said with a grin.

"Clever, babe."

"Anyway, it's not fair because your friends already don't like me and now they're gonna show up and I'm gonna be drunk and stupid."

"Give them twenty minutes and they'll be drunker and stupider," Dave said, patting her leg.

"Har har har," Amy chortled. "I just don't know why they don't like me. And all of you guys just loooove Kara and she's newer than me and she works at Market Basket and I am prettier and I work in insurance."

"I will not argue with any of your points, babe," Dave said, his eyes back on the TV. "C'mon, make 'em throw a lot of pitches!!"

"You won't argue that you all love her more than me?" Amy asked, her eyes trying to focus on Dave's profile.

"Well, I love you more than I love her," Dave said. "Damn it, why'd you swing at that?"

"But why does everyone love Kara and not me?" Amy asked.

"Yes, way to work the pitch count!" Dave yelled as Youk walked to first base. "I'm sorry, what, babe?"

"Why does everyone love Kara and not me?" Amy repeated.

"No one loves Kara more than you," Dave said.

"That's not what you said before..."

Dave studied Amy's unfocused eyes. "Sure it is, babe. Stop being so paranoid. Everyone loves you."

Amy's head rolled back on the couch cushion. "Why am I so druuuuuuunk?"

"You ate that whole container of vodkamelon," Dave recapped, his eyes back on the TV.

"I hate that you didn't tell me it was laced," Amy said.

"Soaked, babe," Dave corrected.

"Whatever," Amy said. "I hate that you let me eat the whole thing."

Dave shrugged. "You were enjoying it."

"But you knew it was gonna fuck me up for when your friends were here and then they'd just laugh at me and hate me more."

"Babe, no one hates you... Yes! Off the wall is a ground rule double!" Dave cheered.

"They hate me because they all still love Samantha and they hate that you dumped her for me."

"Ames, that was like four years ago. No one cares about that anymore."

"But they're all still friends with Samantha, aren't they," Amy said matter-of-factly.

"So what?"

"So what? So what is that they will always wish you were still with her instead of me."

"Babe, that's crazy. Yes! Run! Go! Yes, run scored, that's how we do it, boys!"

"They all wish I was Samantha. I mean, they all wish Samantha was me. I mean, they all wish you still dated Samantha."

"Babe, literally no one still wishes I dated Samantha -- including Samantha."

"How do you know? Did you talk to her?"

Dave sighed. "No, Ames, I just know because I know. Sam's doing her own thing now and she's dating that guy what's-his-name--"

"Kevin," Amy supplied.

"Yeah, right, Kevin. Glasses-guy, that's what I call him in my mind, couldn't think of his real name..."

"Why are you giving Samantha's boyfriend a weird nickname in your head?" Amy asked. "Are you jealous of him?"

"Babe, no, calm down. I dumped her for you, remember?"

"Well, that doesn't mean you're not jealous of him. He's with the perfect Sa-*man*-tha. Everyone loves Sa-*man*-tha. I bet Sa-*man*-tha and *Kara* would be besties and you'd all *love* hanging out with them."

Dave studied her critically. "Vodka turns you crazy," he said finally.

Amy's mouth hung open. "I'm not crazy," she said. "I know everyone likes Samantha better than me and Kara better than me. And the fact that you gave her stupid-Kevin-boyfriend a nickname tells me you've thought about it enough to...well...give him a nickname. So what am I supposed to think?"

"Maybe that I don't care enough about his real name in order to remember it?" Dave suggested.

"No," Amy said. "No, no, it's you that's crazy if you think I'm buying that bridge to China."

"Huh?" Dave asked.

"Just never mind. If you wanted to be with Samantha still, you should have just told me," Amy said, folding her arms across her chest.

"I don't want to be with Samantha."

"Well, your friends wish you were."

"That is universally untrue," Dave said. "Sam's a cool chick, don't get me wrong, but she's not the right girl for me. And my friends all know that, Sam included."

"'*Sam included,*'" Amy mocked. "Why do you know that?"

"Because she told me. Maybe six months after she and I broke up, I ran into her at the gym and she said that she had seen you and me at McBreyer's a few days before and she could see how happy I was. And she told me how happy she was and that she was realizing our breakup was for the best."

"Liar," Amy spat. "No way that bitch was telling you the truth. Girls say sneaky shit like that to make it seem like it's cool just so they can get back on your good side and sabotage the hell outta you."

Dave raised an amused eyebrow. "Oh yeah? That was three and a half years ago, Ames. What exactly has she done to prove she feels differently than she said?"

Amy was stumped. "Retort?" she said after a moment.

Dave put an arm around her. "Listen, Ames, you're drunk and crazy right now. I'll text the gang and tell them not to come over because I got wasted on the vodkamelon --"

"Noooooo," Amy moaned. "They will definitely come right over if you say it's you."

"Good point. OK, I will tell them you are burning pictures of Samantha in the kitchen sink and I've called an exorcist and a psychiatrist to come assist you..."

Amy thwaped his chest with the back of her hand. "Why don't you just go meet them at the bar and I'll just stay here and take a nap?"

Dave looked down at her and smiled. "I'd rather stay here with you."

Amy snuggled in under his arm. "You're sweet."

Dave looked back at the TV. "Nah, I'm just in love with a crazy drunk person."

Amy closed her eyes. "I'll sober up eventually at least."

Dave picked up his phone with his free hand and started texting. "At least," he agreed.

First line by Erik Asmussen

Goat Shirt

I've never been a big fan of goats. See, when I was a kid, my friend Christine's family had a goat farm, which meant they lived in the country -- barns, fields, cows, smells, corn, dirt on the shirt, the works -- so if I wanted to go over and play at her house with all the other kids from my class, I had to wear my junk clothes or deal with Mother having a fucking conniption fit like you didn't know was possible if I came home all messy. I barely had any junk clothes, though -- I lived in a goddamn mansion, compared to everyone else. We had a goddamn pond right in our fucking front yard, for chrissakes!! And a chandelier the size of the goddamn moon right in our foyer. Hell, we had a room we called the *foyer*. Shit, man. Junk clothes?? Who was I kidding! But Christine's was the place to be because we could get messy there and she had a horse we could ride. He was a retired 4H horse so he was super friendly and all that shit. We'd ride that fucker all over the show. And I didn't want to be the only kid at school who didn't get to be part of this fun. So I wore the ugly-ass green sweatpants and Looney Tunes t-shirt Mother bought me to wear to Christine's and had the time of my fucking life the minute I got out of my parents' stuffy ass Caddy and onto the land god intended to be a place of sheer awesome.

Except for those goddamn goats.

This one buddy of mine -- Gino was his name-o -- he was always giving me shit about the Looney Tunes and so one still kinda warm fall day, I just ripped the shirt off and waved it in the air like a goddamn flag. "Fuck you, Gino!" I yelled. Shit, my vocabulary sucked back then. Anyway, I waved it around for a little while and then you know what I did? I folded that piece of shit shirt up like it was the goddamn American flag and placed it carefully, ever so carefully, down on this stump near the driveway, and then I ran around like a goddamn maniac with all the other kids. Shirtless, what the fuck? I was a crazy kid, I swear. And, man, I got dirty that day! But as it turned out, that was the least of my problems. Because that little shit Gino wasn't done with me. Oh, no.

While the rest of us ran around playing Kick the Can, Gino had his beady little eyes on me and my clever retort -- and what I mean by that is taking the goddamn shirt off so he would shut the fuck up, not what I said, which was something an illiterate idiot could come up with -- and when the rest of us were kicking ass and taking names in the game, Gino snuck his skinny ass over to that stump, grabbed my stupid shirt, and then flung it in the goat pen.

Man, I can't even tell you how many international laws he broke with that brass balls move.

One -- we're not allowed near the goats. Christine's family raised those fuckers for marketable reasons, like milk and cheese and baby goats and goat kebabs, probably. Who knows? All I know is we weren't allowed to play with them because they were goods, not toys. Shit. Two -- in addition to being a product for sale, we weren't allowed near the goats because they were mean. Sometimes Christine would come into school with her hand all bandaged up because she tried to pet one or some shit. Three -- anyone who has ever seen a cartoon knows that goats eat fucking everything! Tin cans, man! They eat fucking tin cans. They do not discriminate!

And that shithead threw my shirt into the lion's den. Well, the goat pen, but I think the metaphor still applies constructively.

So guess what happened.

Yeah, I no longer owned a Looney Tunes shirt. Fuck me. And Gino, that jerkoff, he sat over by the pen and watched the goats first trample all over Bugs Bunny & Co and then, as if that wasn't bad enough, they started eating it like was a goddamn surf and turf. It was round about that point when he started hollering for us all to come see -- so we did because we're stupid kids -- and I almost lost my shit. Because Mother was coming to get me in like twenty minutes and I was half-naked and unbelievably filthy. My plan was to hide all the dirt under that godforsaken shirt and try not to track mud around my bathroom after I showered away the evidence.

So that shirt was in the mouth of this big fucker that Christine called Olaf and Olaf and I were in a stare-down of epic proportions. Mano a goat. I didn't even think about it, I just launched myself over the fence and into the goat pen to see if I could salvage the shirt at all. Well, I know that was a bad idea right away -- especially since I landed in some goddamn manure. They still call it manure if it's goat shit, right? Anyway, who fucking knows? I landed in it, that's all that matters. So now I'm shirtless, covered in dirt, and up to my ankles in fecal matter -- see, my vocabulary has found me a way around this manure question. Also, like thirty goats are now staring at me. Olaf, especially, looks pissed. He actually starts running at me with his horns and rams me against the fence. So I fall. In the shit. Shit, man. And! I'm getting my ass kicked by a fucking goat.

All the kids were freaking out by this point, so Christine's mom comes out to see what we're fussing about and by the time she figures out there's an eleven-year-old being mauled by her precious Olaf, I'm barely recognizable. I was like one of those *Lord of the Flies* fuckers -- dirty and wild-eyed. Anyway, somehow, she manages to reach through the fence and coax me back on my feet so she and a few of the other boys, even Gino, helped pull me back to safety. I was also relatively OK despite the savagery of the attack. But, man, did I stink! Christine's mom had to hose me down. And she tried to call Mother, but she must've already been on her way because when she pulled that Caddy into the driveway, she was not prepared for the scenario playing out before her. I thought she was going to pass out when she realized her beloved son was the center of the chaos. Christine's mom, poor woman, she had one hand on the hose pointed at me and one wildly gesturing some half-baked explanation to my mother. Mother just grabbed me, now wet and shitty, and wrapped me in a huge tarp Father insisted we keep in the trunk for emergencies -- that old turd could have never imagined it would be used for this, though, I'm quite sure -- and threw me in the backseat of the car. Man, she was pissed at me. I tried to explain it was Gino's fault, but Mother would have none of it. When we got home, she turned the hose on me one more time before ushering me into the basement where our post-pond-swimming shower stall was. She made me use every kind of soap we had in the house, except for dishwasher soap. Too grainy. But every other fucking kind. And even after all of that, I still stunk for the next two days. Goat shit is potent.

So that was the last time I was allowed to go over to Christine's and play with all of my friends. Those fucking goats ruined my formative years social fun. The event became known as Goat Shirt and lives on as legend to all of my friends -- but it lives on as truth for me. Shit. My glass is empty again. Let's do something about that, shall we?

First line by Joe Kay

A Scene from Vegas

When you're on the Vegas Strip, there's so much eye candy, your retinas get cavities. I see it all the time, guys coming in from Farmville, Nebraska -- Middletown, Kansas -- Anywhere, Ohio -- walking down this street like Minnie Mouse grew up and moved here -- *this* is the place where all of your dreams can come true. And you know what? They're right. There's just one catch: you gotta have the cash. That's the one thing they don't tell you when you're a kid -- your dreams ain't free. And the bigger the dream? The bigger the bill. I should know.

So most people who know me, they call me Marty -- or the more near and dear nickname "McFly" -- but my given name is Carlton Fisk Graham-Martin. Yeah, I was born just after the clock hit midnight on October 22, 1975. Yeah, my parents had an unhealthy love for the Boston Red Sox. Yeah, my mother was a raving lunatic feminist who made sure to hyphenate my name on every possible legal document. I mean, hell, can you imagine the first day of school every year for me? I shoulda worn a sign around my neck explaining the ridiculous nature of my name. No one's ever called me "Carlton" but my mother -- not even my father -- he calls me "Carlton Fisk" -- but at this point everyone thinks it's some weird nickname because everyone knows I'm just plain old Marty from Beverly, Massachusetts. Still got the accent and everything. I learned quick that a lot of the big bosses around here, casino owners, bookies, celebrities, even my weed guy, they all like the sound of a man who can't pronounce his R's quite right. So, hell, I can do the dance and tip my cap and for an extra few bucks spout off a round of *Pahk the cah in the Haaavahd Yahd* if it'll get me in where I want to be. Vegas is about survival for guys like me. I gotta be ready to stick my head in the lion's mouth at any moment.

Especially if the ladies are going to be watching. And they are always watching.

I work for a guy most people just call Bobby -- that's how bad ass he is. He owns a few casinos in town, one big one right on the Strip and that's usually where you find me, bouncing. I'm not a big tough guy like you see at most places. But I'm Boston Irish Catholic -- I have a wicked hot temper and fierce right hook. Who cares if I'm only 5'7", 180? Mostly though, I'm just the nice guy who works the door at The Fells who will let anyone cut to the front of the line for, say, two Benjamins apiece. Ain't got two Benjamins? Hope you're pretty. Otherwise, you ain't getting in the club. Sometimes there are only fifteen people in there tripping out to the house music and the neon strobe lights and the line is a hundred people deep. But by the time midnight rolls around, people are so desperate to get inside, they sometimes hand me three Benjamins or four -- just to see what the fuss is all about.

Bobby loves it. He loves watching me work that door. "You're always so calm and almost apologetic, McFly," he says to me. "You make it seem like this is the only club in Vegas that's worthwhile." Bobby, he's not a bad guy, not like people think. He lets me keep all the cash I earn at the door, too, no questions asked. For a long time, I didn't know why that was and by the time I learned, it was already such a part of my life, I never even considered walking away. See, Bobby, he's not exactly what you might call "street legal." He modifies the law a bit, that's all I mean. Like, for instance, there's a bartender in the club I know by the name of Fiddler -- she's all of five feet tall with the most insane turquoise mohawk you ever saw -- probably made her more like 5'4" -- she's the one you want to see to score some X or acid or whatever -- including a rufie. How fucked up is that, ladies? There's one of your own who will sell some asshole a date rape drug right in this club you just paid at least a hundred bucks to go to. Fiddler's just Bobby's public face for his drug ring -- and a lot of people think that she's pulling one over on him -- I seen people warn her, for Chrissakes, to tell her that messing with Bobby will be her doom. Fiddler's always so cool about it, too. She gets all somber and promises to be careful. It's hilarious. Bobby and me, we watch all the good highlights on the security reel after the last asshole is kicked out of the club for the night. Then I tell him about the one or two people who dole out the same warning to me as they question why I am asking for a hundred bucks for a place whose advertised cover is only twenty.

Who are these assholes? These are the same idiots who got to the movies every Friday night and pay twenty dollars for a popcorn and a soda. How's that 200% markup working for you there, champ?

Vegas ain't no different.

Except that everyone here is pretending this is a fantasy and in our fantasies, we're never Suzie Homemaker -- we're Suzie Sex Kitten. So when I stand outside this club night after night, I watch everyone, men and women alike, parade up and down the Strip like this is the last day of life on this planet and, consequently, will be lived to the max. Me, I almost envy their faith in this town, their belief that Vegas will be worthy of the innuendo behind "What Happens Here, Stays Here." I don't even remember the last time a sight of the Strip gave me chills.

Even when I see a beautiful woman, the kind that turns every head who sees her, my eyes, they don't follow her beyond my straightaway gaze. No more eye-cavities for me. I'm immune to it all. Immune to grown-up Disneyland. Can you imagine that? My next vacation's gonna be a tour of the Rock Hall in Cleveland, Ohio. Maybe there's something new to see somewhere normal. Maybe too much of a good thing is just too much.

First line by Sean OhEigeartaigh

About the Author

An Ohio native, Sarah Wolf moved to Boston in 2002 to earn an MFA in Creative Writing from Emerson College. With a publishing history that spans back to 1994, her most recent publications include the novel *Neverland, Ohio*, the short story collections *Black Ohio Skies* and *Sobriety and Forty-Nine Other Fine Stories*, the poetry volume *There are Phases to These Things*, and the collection of writing *Three Hundred Sixty-five for Two Thousand Eleven*.